To Paulette
Love, Sue

BEYOND THE
BLUE SWING DOORS

BEYOND THE
BLUE SWING DOORS

SUE PACEY

First published in Great Britain in 2018 by

Bannister Publications Ltd
118 Saltergate
Chesterfield
Derbyshire S40 1NG

Copyright © Sue Pacey

ISBN 978-1-909813-43.4

Sue Pacey asserts the moral right to be identified
as the author of this work

A catalogue record for this book is available from the British Library

Typeset in Sabon by Escritor Design, Bournemouth

Printed and bound in Great Britain

This book is dedicated to my beloved sister, Jan.
The tenacity and bravery with which she faces each new day
is all the inspiration I need.

Chapter 1

The stark, white-tiled walls of the casualty department were mirrored with flashes of blue as the siren wailed.

The whole area was illuminated, and for a few seconds everyone froze before instincts took over and adrenalin rushed to vital organs – the fight or flight response. In this case 'fight' meant preparation: drawing up necessary drugs and grabbing outdoor clothing, high visibility jackets and hard hats.

It was the major accident alarm and this was the 'Flying Squad'. Nothing to do with the police – this was the wilds of Derbyshire.

It was my first night working on Casualty. 'Fight' for everyone else maybe, but for me, 'flight'. Surely being so young and inexperienced they'd leave me here as part of the 'B' team, safely in the warm where I couldn't do any damage. This team's job was to clear the department of anyone capable of walking and breathing at the same time, then prepare beds and trolleys to accommodate the incoming wounded.

They *would* leave me here, wouldn't they? After all, I was only just coming to the end of my second year of nurse training.

The siren gave another prolonged wail to signal the three-minute warning when everyone assembled under the draughty roof of the ambulance bay with the two steel coffin-like boxes that held all our equipment. Revving noisily and ready to go were two black taxis. One took the boxes of equipment and the other, the medical staff. These vehicles were retained by the hospital for this purpose. We couldn't waste ambulances just to get us there. There weren't enough of them!

I shivered. Perhaps if I hid in the toilet no one would notice my absence. I made my decision and prepared to creep away. No one would miss a short student nurse who, despite warm clothing, stood shaking in the wind tunnel that was the ambulance bay. A quick glance told me there was no more room in the taxi anyway. I breathed a huge sigh of relief.

Without warning, a large paw-like hand landed on my shoulder with surprising gentleness.

'Come on, little nurse, there's always room for one more inside!' The voice was deep, gruff and heavily accented with a Canadian twang. I froze. It was nothing to do with the icy wind that whipped the leaf-litter into eddies around my feet.

'But there's no more...' I began to protest.

'Yes, there *is* room. You can sit on my knee!'

Before I had time to say anything further, my feet left the ground. Two of the biggest hands I ever saw on a human being deposited me on an equally large lap.

Oh, my God! I'm sat on his knee! I didn't know whether to smile politely or cry. Not daring to turn towards him, I sat rigid, looking straight ahead. He stared into my left ear, no doubt with a smirk at my obvious discomfort. It was the longest twenty minutes of my life and during the journey no one made eye contact and not one word was spoken, probably all biting their bottom lip to avoid laughing.

His lap was exceedingly warm and I daren't allow my imagination to question the reason for the increased blood flow that made it so. There was I sat on the knee of the most notoriously grumpy consultant in the hospital, and what was worse he seemed to be enjoying it. I wasn't!

The taxi set off at speed with us packed in like sardines. In the event of an accident, I doubt any of us would have moved far. That was fortunate as seatbelts hadn't been fitted in those days.

So, my first contact – far too intimate for my liking – had occurred with our casualty consultant, Sir Ivor Gagnon. What an introduction. But no one would ever have dreamed of introducing themselves to him. You spoke when, and if, you were spoken to and certainly didn't offer a friendly word or your hand, unless you wanted it bitten off! His fierce reputation preceded him. He was *the* boss and that was obvious the first time you heard him bellow 'Nurse!' at full throttle.

The taxi slowed as we approached what looked from a distance like a fairground. The myriad of flashing lights brought everyone quickly back to reality. This was Junction 29 of the recently opened M1 motorway and there had been a horrendous accident. Carnage was an inadequate word to describe the sight we saw as we stepped out onto the carriageway.

Vehicles littered the north side across all three lanes, lit by a few still-functioning headlights and the arc lights the fire brigade had brought with them. Two cars were lying upside down resting on their roofs with glass smashed everywhere and twisted metal sticking out at impossible angles. There was a lorry ablaze on its side. It lay at right angles across all three lanes. There was nothing left of its load, and little remained except the chassis.

'Bloody hell!' exclaimed Dan Todburgh, the casualty registrar who was standing beside me. He put out his arm. 'Stay well behind me, Nurse and don't get too close in case there's anything left in the fuel tank to blow up. Stay on the hard shoulder with all the gear until you're told what to do.' I didn't need telling twice.

One look at all the other wrecked vehicles with their invariably dead and seriously injured occupants was enough. I began to open the metal trunks in readiness, then started to assemble intra-venous sets, fitting needles to syringes in readiness for drugs to be drawn up. Time would be of the essence for some of the injured. Speed and efficiency was what was needed.

I watched my experienced colleagues as they got to work, awestruck at their calmness in the face of such adversity – not unlike automatons on a production line. Unlike me, *they* had seen it all before. There must have been in excess of forty vehicles involved, stretching away into the distance with police and firefighters blending into the blur before my eyes.

Before long, there was a row of bodies covered with black plastic sheeting laid out on the grassy banking that skirted the motorway, as if to give protection against the driving rain and hail which was now falling – and some dignity in death. I turned my head away and tried to concentrate on the job despite cold, numb fingers and trembling hands. My paper cap had been discarded in favour of a hard, white hat bearing a red cross. Mascara ran in rivulets down my cheeks. It was not all the rain's doing.

A fireman appeared carrying the body of a small boy. The

man was weeping, no doubt thinking of his own little ones safely tucked up in their beds. Despite the cold, he began to unbutton his jacket to wrap around the child. Quickly I grabbed a blanket and ran towards him.

'No,' I cried. 'Put it back on, *you* need that! Let me do it.' I held out the blanket and he placed the child in my arms. 'I'll take care of him. I promise.' He appeared stunned and rooted to the spot, a look of sheer helplessness on his face. I shouted louder, my voice almost lost above the noise of the generators and cutting equipment. 'I'll look after him.'

I laid the child, who couldn't have been more than four, on the embankment and swaddled him in the soft blanket. I spoke to him softly. There wasn't a mark on him. I supposed he must have broken his neck in the impact. 'Come on little chap,' I said. 'You have a sleep now.'

I looked back. The fireman was still standing there, shocked. I walked over to him and touched his arm. His body jerked and he gasped, the human contact wrenching him from his stupor. He looked at me with eyes that mirrored pain.

'Go back,' I said. 'They need you.'

He turned and ran into the blur of lights, heavy rain and horror.

I don't remember much about the journey back to the hospital, but I *do* remember the silence, overwhelming sadness and a sense of hopelessness as we pulled in to the ambulance bay. The wind had dropped and the rain lessened in deference to the solemnity of the occasion.

All the wounded, both walking and those on stretches, had arrived before us. There were nine dead and many more injured who'd been diverted to hospitals in nearby cities. One casualty department could only cope with so many. As it was, every single bay in ours was full, with trolleys occupying the corridor.

In the waiting area, I had a few precious minutes to myself before joining the melee on the other side of the blue swing doors of the casualty department. I needed to change into dry scrubs before I caught my death of cold. Some kind soul had pressed a mug of tea into my icy hands and I was determined to drink it whatever. For now, I was alone and cocooned with my thoughts, standing in front of the fish tank that kept so many children entertained in the daytime while they waited to be seen.

The waiting hall was abandoned. It had been quickly cleared of people in line with our major accident policy. My hapless reflection in the glass tank told the whole story. I watched the fish going about their daily business, sucking at the gravel to harvest algae, keeping all things as they should be. In the corner of the tank, a grey fairy castle provided a hiding place when small faces pressed too close against the glass. I watched as the bubbles rose upwards and broke on the surface. Oxygen! Life-giving air. My mind drifted back to the dark, wet road where so many had no need of it any more.

How fragile life is! How fragile was theirs! They had no way of knowing this was their last day on earth. Lost on a rain-drenched, icy road in the Midlands, some far from home and loved ones; a road to nowhere except oblivion. Who were they? Where were they going? What were their hopes and dreams?

I breathed deeply on the air-filled oxygen that no longer needed to be shared with them and, running my fingers through rain-soaked hair, closed my eyes for a moment until a firm hand on my arm brought me rushing back to the present.

'Drink your tea, Paola. We must get on. Now go and shower. There's a lot to do.' I turned to see who the voice belonged to. There was no one.

Swallowing the now-cooling drink in one gulp and discarding the cup, I walked quickly into the shower room to the left of the blue swing doors with no backward glance in the direction of the voice.

Chapter 2

The dead child was called Joshua Frazer and his parents and baby sister had all been badly injured in the crash. The boy had been thrown from the car and, as I suspected, broken his neck. He died instantly.

At some time during the past year, I'd stopped asking 'Why?' I really can't remember at what point it happened. It crept up on me, I suppose. Ever since the love of my life, Robbie, had been killed in Vietnam, I'd been too consumed with my own grief to feel that of others or even to empathise with their suffering. He'd been brought back to me for a few brief moments one night in the kitchen and I'd found it comforting – for a time. I still felt his loss deeply and it was often so raw that sometimes I felt I might die too.

But nothing is as simple as that. There *is* no easy way out of grief, no shortcut to acceptance of tragedy and no quick fix to dispel the pain. The fact that I was a medium was of little comfort. It had taken a very long time for me to accept it, but with Robbie's help, I had. I could see and hear the dead and there was no getting away from it. It was as normal to me as breathing, and if less enlightened folk thought me odd it was their problem. I couldn't hide or deny it any longer because I didn't want to. Robbie had taught me to cherish the gift I'd been given. *That* was the easy part. I was stuck with it. I'd cherished him, not always understanding his motives and reasoning, but what woman really *does* understand a man? With his death in the skies over Vietnam, he'd become just another number on a dog tag, another casualty of that dreadful war to everyone. Everyone but me. I'd taken my so-called gift and begun to listen with new intensity. Robbie believed in me. I was not about to sully his memory by not believing in myself.

Bereavement is isolating. The way some people deal with loss is to give space – whatever that means. Some try to carry on as normal and ignore the fact that the person died or pretend they never existed at all. It doesn't work like that! There were those who crossed the road rather than speak to me, presumably in case I broke down in tears. They were afraid they wouldn't know what to say. Well let me tell you, anything is better than saying nothing because *that* feels like a further insult.

Having been subjected to this treatment, I made a vow never to fail to acknowledge anyone in this position because it compounds the pain. To be ignored is so much more isolating. I longed for them to say something, even if it was only 'What the hell are you wearing?' or 'You look like shit, girl'. I didn't want pity or a crass comment like, 'I know what you're going through' because they didn't. What I *did* need was inclusion. Not all the time, but just to be allowed to cry when I wanted and to laugh without feeling guilty. I wanted to do all the things that normal people do without anyone pussyfooting around treating me like a fragile rosebud about to fall apart. I loved him, couldn't they see that? I didn't want to forget him or put him to the back of my mind. I wanted what I couldn't have – and that was Robbie's arms around me. So, I had to have the next best thing – the memory of it. I needed to play it over and over in my head trying to remember every detail, afraid that one day it would be gone. He'd invaded my life, my soul and my every waking moment and he was still there in the background of my days and in the foreground of my nights. I was paying the price for loving him in the same way all things must be paid for. I felt battered and broken and could never imagine feeling good again. It's called the grieving process.

Shelagh was the one person who understood. My zany, Irish friend. I bless the day I met her!

Having endured the dubious pleasure of sitting on Sir Ivor's lap for twenty minutes too long, I somehow managed to avoid our consultant for the next few days. I ran errands no one else wanted to do and volunteered for the worst job in the department – cleaning all the trolley wheels. I could literally keep my head down and go unnoticed by anyone important. But it couldn't last.

June Lowry, our rather long-in-the-tooth staff nurse, was moving on. She'd worked at Sir Ivor's side for ten years and somehow managed to remain sane. Until a willing soul was found to fill her considerable shoes, there was to be a shortfall. I couldn't imagine anyone volunteering to replace her and envisaged it was going to be a very long shortfall!

She followed me into the staffroom on her last day and uncharacteristically made me a cup of coffee, patting the seat beside her. 'Sit down, Nurse. I've something to tell you. Do you take sugar?'

'Err...no thanks.' I was getting worried.

'Well, you know it's my last day today.' I nodded, hoping she wasn't expecting a present. 'I'm leaving and for the next week...well, anyone can survive a *week*, can't they?' She paused for me to catch up, but I was still bemused. '*You*, my dear, will be taking over...assisting him... Sir Ivor.' Her voice trailed off.

Reality dawned, my eyes saucer-like. 'No! Nononononono – but I'm only a student. I couldn't possibly assist *him*.' The last word came out *sotto voce*. I began to panic, my voice getting higher with each plea. 'Nurse Lowry, help me! Say it's a joke. It *is* a joke, isn't it?' I could sense her pity.

'You'll be fine.' She patted my hand and I spilled the coffee.

'But, Nurse Lowry...June.' I was begging now. 'Please...he kills people!'

'No, my pet,' she whispered, 'not often, and only if they don't duck quickly enough.'

'Aaaah,' I groaned, head in my hands. 'Do you suppose if I appealed to Matron it might help?'

'Not a chance, I'm afraid. They're like that!' She linked her little fingers to emphasise the strength of the relationship. 'This is my last day and,' she consulted her watch, 'I am now officially retired.'

'I'm happy for you!' I wailed. 'Really I am, but couldn't you just stay on for another month? I'm moving to Bamford Ward then.' Frantically, I tried to mop spilt coffee from the front of my uniform dress.

June Lowry closed her eyes and uttered a deep sigh. 'By then, my dear, I shall be aboard the QE2 on the way to America to visit my sister. He's all yours I'm afraid. Paola, it's only for a week. Seven short days!'

'But he throws things!' I was nearly sobbing.

'Well, you must learn to duck,' she said. 'Don't answer back and remember he hates hot water bottles with a passion, so it's wise to give the blankets a good frisk when patients come in.' She stood and put on her coat. 'Oh, and make sure he has a clean, white coat each morning and coffee at eleven sharp, black with three sugars.' She picked up her bag and left, shooting me a look of sheer pity. Then, as a parting shot she whooped, 'USA, here I come!'

I sat in complete misery. I'd been looking forward to a rare weekend off, but it had just lost its rosy glow. First thing Monday morning I was to become the personal assistant and dogsbody to the fiercest, most irascible and humourless consultant in the hospital. If ever there was a way to spoil a weekend, it just happened.

I returned to the nurses' home in search of Shelagh with the intention of dragging her out to the nearest pub. If I was going to die during the following week, I intended to have a damn good time first. We were going to dress to the nines, feed the juke box and get rolling drunk before the landlord of the Shakespeare pub threw us out, disorderly and singing into the street. Word would then get back to Matron. I'd be sacked on the spot and wouldn't have to go to work on Monday after all. If that failed, I would pray that by some miracle the whole thing would go away.

The Lord was obviously otherwise engaged so, at seven o'clock on Monday morning I presented myself for duty. As the weekend had progressed, I'd become a little more philosophical, perhaps due to the alcohol. It was *only* for a week. He was *only* a man like all other men. I could *do* this. What could *possibly* go wrong?

I peered around the door to the waiting area. It was already starting to fill with people. We had a system – if you could call it that. It was first-come first-served, and on arrival everyone was issued with a number to avoid any fighting. The only exceptions were anyone who wasn't breathing, severely haemorrhaging or unconscious.

At 7.30am on the dot, the blue swing doors would be opened

to let in the hoards, and we would work until every single person had been seen. But before that, at precisely 7.29am, those same doors would be flung open with a loud crash sending paint chips flying, as in marched the man-mountain that was Sir Ivor, and in his wake his junior and registrar. Both had to run to keep up with him. He was 'Sir' and no one had the nerve to address him otherwise. Once inside he strode towards his office leaving the doors rattling on their hinges. A great bellow of 'Nurse' signalled I was about to meet my fate. I tapped on the door that bore his nameplate.

'Enter!' he boomed again. 'What are you waiting for – an invitation?' I swallowed hard and went inside. 'Oh, ho, ho,' he guffawed. 'Well, if it isn't my little lap pet.' I smiled inanely. He reminded me of Santa Claus with his bushy, almost white, beard and unruly mop of matching hair. Black eyes peered out from the thicket, sharp enough to have cut you down. But this was no benevolent, gift-toting uncle. I took in the huge paw-like hands and feet so large he'd have been well-anchored in a force-nine gale. For a few seconds I was unable to take my eyes from them, wondering how he managed to get shoes to fit – a canoe builder perhaps? I must have smiled because the windows rattled to a howl of 'Wipe that smile off your face and give me my coat, girl.'

I looked at his two juniors on the other side of the desk.

'Go on!' mouthed Joe James, the registrar indicating frantically towards the back of the door. The look on his face pleaded. *For God's sake, don't upset him this early in the morning.*

Taking the fresh, white coat from the peg where I'd hung it earlier, I held it out at arm's length. Sir Ivor glowered and walked slowly towards me never taking his eyes from my face. He paused directly in front of me, eyebrows raised in a question to which I clearly didn't know the answer. Slowly he turned his back.

'Nurse, my coat.'

'Oh...' Daylight dawned. He wanted me to hold the coat, so he could slip it on. *Why can't he just bloody-well say that?* Now here was a problem. I'm four feet ten inches tall and he's six feet eight – nearly two feet taller. The logistical problem was obvious. Either I would have to stand on a chair or he would have to bend down almost to his knees. And I was *not* about to go climbing on any chairs. If he wanted to wear that coat he could damn well

11

put it on himself. Oh, the folly of youth! I saw the juniors wince.

Sir Ivor stood for a few moments, then, with no action forthcoming, slowly turned with a huff and fixed me with a stare that could have soured milk. He grabbed the coat, threw it around his large body and buttoned it while still glowering down at me. 'A small victory on this occasion, my little lap pet.' A dismissive wave told me I should go.

I went – at speed. But from that day he put on his own coat!

Mercifully, I was spared further contact for the rest of the day. I was assigned to 'minors' and was far too busy to even look over my shoulder. This room was where all the minor injuries were seen. Joe James and Ralph Law, the junior house officers, were more than capable of dealing with the cuts, bruises and those who needed diverting to the X-ray department. I proved my worth with some deft bandaging when they'd finished stitching. It quickly became my job to see all the small children who'd swallowed stuff they shouldn't have – coins and suchlike. Children seem to have an absolute preoccupation for shoving objects into openings in their bodies where objects aren't meant to be shoved. I was astonished at the diversity of stuff that we'd removed from ears and noses.

One little boy presented us with a challenge. Following an X-ray, it was clear to see he'd inserted his favourite toy soldier up his nose. Such was the clarity of the film that the soldier appeared to be saluting. So, with a lot of reassurance and a quick shot of anaesthetic spray, it was rapidly removed with nasal forceps by Joe before the child could protest. The toy was wiped and returned to his mother who gave him a slap to ensure there wouldn't be a repeat performance. It would most likely end up at the very bottom of the toy box or hidden away where he couldn't find it again.

The following days passed quickly in much the same way and I began to relax. I'd made it to Friday without incurring the wrath of Sir Ivor, whilst earning respect from the doctors with my ability to quieten small children, and my bandaging skills were becoming legendary. And because I often brought in cake.

I'd begun to bake after Robbie's death for something to do, filling the nurses' home with delicious smells. It was very therapeutic and amazing how many people just happened to call into the kitchen on their way to somewhere else. Our mother had seen to it that her offspring were all able to cook and sew, in the hope we'd impress someone enough to take each of us off her hands one day. What more did she want? With four daughters, she'd ensured herself constant help in the kitchen, because looking back to the 1950s the sexes had much more defined roles. Women didn't mend cars or go to football matches and men didn't cook, darn socks or turn shirt collars. We still lived in a 'make do and mend' society long after the war was won. When I'd left for nurse training, Mum had presented me with my very own Be-Ro cookery book. The pictures were all in brown and white and I still have it to this day. It represented the cook's bible.

Every few days after work, I'd set to and bake a cake to put in the staff room on Casualty for everyone to share. The junior doctors were like gannets, and each day as I came on duty they would be looking for what I'd brought in and suffering from a bad case of premature salivation as coffee time approached. We never offered Sir Ivor any as, being only one step away from the Almighty, it was beneath him to take his coffee with us lesser mortals. His office door stayed firmly closed until he'd drained the last drop and a bellow of 'Nurse' signalled break-time was well and truly over.

I'd a whole weekend off to look forward to and practically skipped as I made my way back to the nurses' home down the steep slope past the mortuary, or 'Ivy Cottage' as it was known.

They stood in the shadows thrown out by the wall and its canopy: two lovers embracing. Strong arms protected a diminutive woman who, with her head against his chest, was crying. Not a wail, but a gentle, dignified sob. *These* were no lovers, but a couple lost in their private grief. Casting my eyes down I walked past, feeling like the man in the Bible who passed by on the other side. I was trying to be as unobtrusive as possible. Before I went down the steps to the nurses' home I glanced back to check they were okay and was surprised to see the woman staring after me. Our eyes met and I took a few steps forward.

'Are you okay?' I asked softly.

She looked at me sadly, her lips quivering, tear-stained cheeks flushed with emotion. 'Nurse,' she whispered. 'Did you see him? Did you see my child?' I took a couple more steps towards her, aware they were outside the mortuary at dusk. 'My boy,' she pleaded reaching out for me. 'His name is Joshua.'

'I'm sorry,' I began, 'I'm afraid not. Is he...'

'I can't find him. Please help me find him.' The despair in her eyes was heart-breaking.

'I'll do all I can,' I said. 'I'm just going to the nurses' home to get rid of my bag and then we'll look together.'

She turned and placed her head against the black woollen coat of her companion and sighed. His face was in shadow and all I could see was a man's hand wearing a wedding ring as he gently stroked her hair.

I hurried to the nurses' home, threw my bag inside the porch and ran back up the steps to the mortuary. They'd lost their child. It was obvious, and nothing could change that. But I could find someone more senior to help, if they wished to go inside to see the boy. I couldn't leave these grieving parents on one side of the cold, ivy-clad wall whilst their son lay on the other. I reached the door, but they were gone. I looked around with a sigh. Perhaps they weren't ready to see him yet and returned home to grieve behind closed doors where the world couldn't witness their pain.

Though desperately weary, I couldn't sleep. The sight of that poor couple went on invading my mind. Despite trying to relax, back they came, the crying woman and the faceless man in the dark coat. With a grunt of resignation, I climbed out of bed and put on my dressing gown and slippers. It was 1am and the building was silent. Spooning cocoa into hot milk, I found myself smiling, remembering another such night.

I'd first got to know Robbie over two mugs of cocoa in this very kitchen. Being an American, he'd called it 'chocolate', and that night a spark had been lit. It was still smouldering.

The resident cat, Mitch, sat in her favourite spot on the boiler purring, with one eye open for the odd passing mouse no doubt. The moment I sat, she took it as her cue to move. She stretched, yawned and jumped noiselessly onto my lap. I sipped cocoa and stroked her, comfortable in the soft shadows with memories threatening to bring back feelings still hard to bear. Love, passion and loss. Closing my eyes with the warm mug pressed against my cheek, I wondered how so much could have happened since I first walked into this building. Oh, Pao! I remonstrated, this is no good. Returning the cat to her roost and rinsing the mug, I went wearily back to my room. It was hopeless. Why is it I can't sleep when I'm so tired?

Thoughts raced, one memory triggering another, and there was a cacophony of voices in my head I didn't want to listen to – at least not tonight. So, dressing warmly and pulling on my boots, I did what I always did at times like these.

Before Robbie's death, if King Kong had climbed into bed with me, I wouldn't have woken up. Now I missed the warmth and closeness of a man's body, lonely and isolated in my little room. No amount of alcohol or sleeping pills ever helped. The radio in the early hours offered the odd play and music suited to the over seventies, who presumably couldn't sleep either! So, I took up walking. It might have seemed foolhardy, a woman alone in the middle of the night but I *was* aware of my safety. I followed a route along the road in well-lit areas. It's amazing what you see at that time of night. I knew exactly who was doing what – and with whom.

By 3am, I'd done my usual route and was heading back. My walk took me past a lake where a couple of lads fished all night whatever the weather! I was such a familiar sight we'd wave to each other. Happy with life, I walked on until a vehicle suddenly drew up alongside me.

'Morning lass,' said the police officer in the passenger seat. 'Okay, are we?'

The use of the plural always irritated me and I scowled. '*We* are fine, thanks Officer.'

'So where are you off to this early, eh luv?'

'For a walk,' I said, with ill-disguised irritation, as though it were the most natural activity in the world. 'Do I look like a burglar?'

He glared at me with obvious disapproval.

Perhaps he thinks I'm a prostitute on a slow night. 'Really, I'm fine.' I carried on walking, aware the car was creeping after me. It caught up.

'Hop in, luv. We'll give you a lift home.'

I was getting miffed now. They were beginning to look like kerb-crawlers.

'That *won't* be necessary,' I retorted. 'Look, I can't sleep, so I walk. Is that okay?'

'Why? Have you got problems, luv?'

'Only sleeping,' I growled between clenched teeth, all attempts at politeness abandoned.

'We're only thinking of your safety, luv. Can't you take the dog with you?'

I stopped, turned and addressed them through the window. 'I don't have a dog, Officer. I've a cat, but she won't come. The minute I open the door, she's back on the bed like a shot.'

'Perhaps you should join her!' The policeman's eyes narrowed.

'Officer, *please* don't worry about me. I can look after myself.'

The car came to an abrupt halt and seven feet of uniform got out and opened the rear door. 'Get in, lady and stop messing us about.' It was not a request. They were clearly under the impression I'd escaped from somewhere, and not wanting to be arrested, did as I was told.

Oh God, they're taking me back to the nurses' home in a police car! I hope everyone's still asleep. The custodians of the law were not satisfied until they'd seen me in through the boiler house, not understanding why I didn't just ring the front doorbell. They clearly hadn't met Tissie, our venerable home sister. Miss Thistlethwaite: temple guardian, self-appointed Rottweiler and custodian of the virginity of 'her girls'. If I'd gone in the front door the game would've been up, and with it a fond farewell to late passes until next Michaelmas, at least.

So, after navigating the boiler room, I reached the main staircase on tiptoe, toying with the idea of going out again. *Nah, they'd probably be parked up somewhere with their lights off lying in wait.* Those two and Tissie would've made a good team.

Pausing at the bottom of the staircase, I bent to remove my walking boots and busy with the laces didn't hear the approach. A pink dressing-gowned figure caught my eye as I stood, my eyes taking in the tartan zipped slippers with pom-poms. One foot was tapping rhythmically. My eyes travelled upwards to a face white with cream, thin, peevish mouth and black gimlet eyes. On top were large pink rollers and a hairnet. I froze.

'Nurse Green!' It was a bellow like a bull.

She wasn't bothered about waking the occupants of the building. I winced.

'*What* may I ask is the meaning of this? Well?' Temporarily lost for words I opened and closed my mouth like a stranded salmon. 'My office at ten sharp. Do *not* be late.'

'Yes, Miss Thistlethwaite.' My voice was a mere whisper.

'Now get to bed!' she spat, arms folded, her foot still tapping.

I went, and quickly climbed into bed pulling the covers up around my neck.

'Now doesn't that just serve you right, clever clogs?' said a voice close to my left ear.

'Oh, go away,' I pleaded and then more forcefully, 'nobody likes a smart Alec!' There was a ripple of laughter that stayed in the room for a few moments. Then, I slept.

Chapter 3

Next morning in Tissie's office, I was given the roasting of my life.

Where had I been? Who with and why? Didn't I know there were evil people around? What was I thinking going out alone at that hour? It went on and on. Then, I was docked a month's worth of late-passes and told to behave myself as she'd be watching my every move. I didn't doubt it.

I'll never know how she managed to find out I'd been hauled home in a police car. She had some sort of finely-tuned radar, instinctively knowing when there was something underhand going on – like a mother hen knows when one of her brood is missing. She possessed a phenomenon unexplained by science. I just had to accept that for the next month, Saturday nights were to be spent alone in my room with a good book.

There was another sort of advanced communication that existed in the nurses' home and that was the 'bush telegraph'. Within twenty-four hours everyone knew about the wayward nurse who'd gone wandering around the countryside at 3am and had been brought home in a police car. With repeated telling, the story had been embellished from Paola Green going for a stroll, to Paola Green obviously supplementing her pay by going 'on the game'. Dressed to the nines and drunk, she'd been arrested and brought home in handcuffs.

I tried to ignore it all but judging by the looks of admiration from some quarters, it had clearly enhanced my reputation for sheer guts, if nothing else. It was a long weekend and I was almost glad to return to Casualty on Monday morning.

Just one more week to get through, Pao. What can possibly go wrong in a week?

'Nurse!' A thunderous roar brought me running from the autoclave room where I'd been sterilising instruments ready for the morning invasion.

'Yes, Sir Ivor. I'm coming.'

He sat behind his large oak desk, wearing a clean white coat which, after all these years, he'd managed to put on himself. He was smirking. 'Well if it isn't Mademoiselle Green!' He cocked an eyebrow and gave the juniors a knowing look. Gentlemen, if what Home Sister tells me is correct, then our Nurse Green here is building quite a reputation for breaking the rules. *We* are to keep her on the straight and narrow while she's in this department.' I shuffled. 'Stand still, girl! So, *this* young woman feels she's invincible.' He carried on talking about me as if I wasn't there. I cleared my throat. 'And so, let's see just how invincible she *really* is. She will be my scrub nurse this morning.' I gave an audible gulp. 'We have a burr holes to perform on an unfortunate motorcyclist who parted company with his infernal machine and landed on his head.'

Oh no! I'm to assist him in the trauma theatre. I knew there'd be another sister there, but *I* would be standing next to him. His bad temper whilst operating was legendary. I wanted to cry.

'So, my little lap pet, I suggest you go and scrub up.' A dismissive wave sent me scurrying to get ready. He had never allowed a mere student to assist him in his beloved trauma theatre before, *and* for the mega-serious surgery that was a burr holes. My heart was hammering.

When someone suffers a severe head injury, several things happen. The brain rattles around inside the skull and it's this prolonged movement that causes the damage. Normally the skull's strong cage protects the fragile structures deep within the brain that control movement, our thought processes, memory and emotions. Operating on it is a highly-skilled and delicate job.

Under the theatre sister's watchful eye, I scrubbed up as I'd been taught, paying special attention to my nails and finger webbing. Then, I walked into my proffered gown and put on sterile gloves using the 'no touch' technique.

Sister smiled and nodded her approval. 'Well done, Nurse Green. Now let's check our instruments for this procedure. Do those gloves fit, by the way?'

'Yes, thank you, Sister.' She'd had to send a porter to the children's ward to get a pair small enough to fit my size-five hands. The same thoughtful porter had also brought me a box to stand on, so I could see over the operating table. We checked the instruments and placed them on the trolley in order of need.

There were sponge holders for swabs to clean the skin after it had been shaved; scalpels of different sizes; Spencer-Wells forceps to peel back any layers of fat and stem bleeding, and finally, a drill to remove a portion of the bone. There were further fine scalpels to cut the delicate membrane that protected the brain, and screwdrivers to put it all back together again. It resembled the kind of tool kit needed to erect a fence and not an extremely delicate brain operation to save a man's life. The whole point was to release the dangerous pressure build-up within the brain. When we hurt ourselves, the area swells to protect damaged tissues. But the skull fuses when we reach adulthood and so that swelling has nowhere to go. Brain function is quickly compromised.

If we don't intervene, confusion and stupor occur leading to unconsciousness as vital pathways are interrupted. Breathing becomes depressed and fits occur from the disrupted messages of a swollen brain. If there's bleeding, it's much worse. A sensitive engine can't operate if it's covered in goo. That's where *our* intervention comes in – to limit the damage and restore that function. That is why head injuries in children are often better tolerated due to the soft spots – the fontanelles. Isn't nature wonderful? It's as though she knows kids are always falling over.

Like a galleon in full rig, Sir Ivor sailed into theatre, gown flapping in his wake. In his well-practised way Tom Banks, the theatre technician and general dogsbody, caught up with him, tying the gown securely without his need to break stride. Sir Ivor surveyed his kingdom and grunted, gloved hands held aloft. 'Right, ladies and gentlemen, shall we begin?'

The unfortunate patient, unconscious since the accident was transferred to the operating table and his airway taken over by the anaesthetist. After surgery he would be kept asleep for days or weeks before being gradually woken. His body was now completely covered, apart from the small shaved area on top of his head.

'Humph!' Sir Ivor retorted. 'Bloody motorbikes. Should be banned from the roads. They're sodding death traps.' He looked directly at me and I bit my lip. It didn't require a reply.

Banned; along with hot water bottles and short, infamous student nurses, since I'd clearly been added to his hate-list.

Without further comment, he held out his gloved palm purposefully in my direction. Taking a deep breath, I placed sponge holders and a swab deftly in his hand, handles first.

'Nurse Green, you appear to have grown.' Any smile was hidden by the folds of his linen mask and had not reached his eyes. I concentrated hard on my part of the job. 'Scalpel!' The detachable blade had already been fixed by Sister – apparently not too well. It fell off as I picked it up.

'Sorry.' I addressed the huge, waiting palm while I attached another with shaking hands.

He began to operate. I looked at Sister who gave me a reassuring look. She was probably thinking something completely different. There was absolute silence except for my heart hammering. I was sure everyone else could hear it. The drill whirred into life accompanied by a horrendous smell of singed bone. Swallowing hard, I fought a wave of nausea. Two large holes were drilled in the skull and he held out his hand for a fine scalpel to excise the dural membrane. Reaching in, he pulled out a dark red clot – a subdural haematoma – the result of bleeding.

'There we are. That's the bugger. Now let's close. Scissors!' I breathed a huge sigh of relief and handed him the wrong pair. He stared at them for a moment. 'No!' he boomed. 'Stitch scissors.'

I fumbled on the trolley, panic rising. Where were they? With a roar, he threw the offending scissors at the wall, one blade penetrating halfway up. They stuck there and quivered like an arrow just missing the passing theatre orderly – *only* just!

That was it. I could put up with his insults, but he'd gone too far. He'd almost skewered poor Tom Banks to the wall by his ear. I turned on him and our eyes met. Reason left me, and at that moment I couldn't have cared less who he was. 'You...stupid man. You should be ashamed of yourself.' I spat out each word to stunned silence, everyone else having frozen. My lip quivered more from temper than fear. I gripped the stitch scissors tightly.

Sir Ivor leaned forward and whispered in my ear. 'Are you going to give me those?'

My eyes narrowed. At that second, I'd have dearly loved to have stuck them in him to see how *he* liked it, but instead slapped them in the palm of his hand. Poor Sister's head visibly retreated into her shoulders like a startled tortoise anticipating disaster. She gently moved me aside and took over. I fell off my box and ran, stumbling to the staff room where I ripped off my theatre 'greens' and burst into angry tears. It was more to do with lack of control than what could have befallen Tom Banks. I waited miserably for retribution that never came. That was the worst. I felt like a condemned prisoner with no fixed execution date.

At eleven o'clock I emerged, peering carefully around each corner for signs or sound of Sir Ivor.

Casualty was heaving with people. When the consultant was dealing with a serious emergency, there was no deputy to take over the routine cases. What the juniors were unable to handle just had to wait. This had been the case and the queue stretched around the waiting room, out of the doors and across the car park.

The Dooleys were a well-known Romany family, their reputation preceding them wherever they pitched their caravans. In the 1920s, a reign of terror across the south of England had seen them chased from every county by the local constabularies. They'd settled in rural Derbyshire.

Though diminished in numbers by lost fights to the death and incarceration over the years, the family was still considerable. It was led by a formidable matriarch, Meghan Dooley, from a small fleet of caravans just off the motorway – presumably for a quick getaway should the need arise. This branch of the family was made up of six sons and three daughters. The men were engaged in numerous dubious activities involving buying and selling scrap metal. It was the women who were the problem. They were all prostitutes with Meghan at the helm and still very active as a working girl herself, reputed to 'do owt for half a crown!' When the weekend came, the whole lot of them would get drunk and fight.

The blue swing doors shot open like a saloon bar scattering paint and rattling on their hinges. In stomped a hugely-proportioned woman in the shortest of skirts. Black suspenders, visible below its hem, held up torn, black fishnet stockings. Yellowing blonde hair fluttered behind her like a ragged curtain as she came in. She sported two swollen black eyes, a lacerated lip and apparently no teeth. The doors still reverberated as she trudged in her biker's boots towards Sir Ivor's office.

'Excuse me…' I ran forward and blocked her way. 'I'm afraid you'll have to join the queue,' I said. 'These people have been waiting all morning.'

She glowered down at me, hands on hips and uttered two words. 'Bleedin' shift!'

I was taken aback and looked around for support. Why was no one protesting? They were all simply looking at the ground.

'No…wait,' I began. With a toothless guffaw, she shoved past me with such force I almost fell over. In several huge strides, she'd reached the office door. I watched open-mouthed as she pushed it open and marched in, with a loud 'Mornin' boss!'

I looked around. Shoulders were being shrugged and *still* no one was complaining.

Okay I thought, and loitered outside the door to await the explosion. It was quiet and after about five minutes the door opened gently and Sir Ivor stood framed in the doorway.

'Ah, Nurse Green,' he said amicably as though nothing had happened. 'Do come in. This is Mrs Meghan Dooley and I'd be grateful if you'd take her and clean her eyes and then I'll come and stitch her up. She got into a small altercation last night, didn't you, Meghan?'

Meghan nodded and wiped her nose on her sleeve. 'Tha should see t'other bloke, doc."

'Now,' he said quietly, patting her shoulder, 'you go with my Nurse Green here.'

My eyebrows took on a mind of their own all but disappearing beneath my fringe as Meghan paused to look directly at me through half-closed, swollen lids.

'Green…. Green? I know thee!' She waved a grubby finger an inch from my nose and for a moment I thought she was going

24

to hit me. 'Aren't tha Joe Green's lass – from off Derby Road?'

'Yes…that's right.' I nodded. 'That's my dad.'

Sir Ivor's mouth fell open.

'Fuckin' hell! Joe Green's lass – no mistakin' them eyes.' She leaned forward and peered at me. 'Nah…if ever tha's in trouble lass, thee just come and find Meghan and…' She rolled up her sleeve revealing muscles a navvy would have been proud of, 'they'll get some o'this. I'll knock their bleedin' 'eads off!'

Sir Ivor folded his arms and leaned on the door frame watching as she went calling to right and left, 'Well, pittle me pants! I know this little lass. Joe Green's she is – and she's a good 'un!'

I followed her. What would everyone think? That I was a trainee prostitute in my spare time? God forbid! How else could I have known Meghan Dooley? My face remained flushed for the rest of the day. It was not helped one iota when Sir Ivor eventually caught up with me as I was about to go off duty.

'My goodness, Nurse Green, I suspected you were a woman of varied talents.' He winked and I fled.

I never did get around to asking my father how he came to be acquainted with Meghan Dooley, who policemen used to turn up in pairs to arrest. Sometimes, it's better not to know!

It was over. My stint on Casualty was over. I'd survived – just. I'd managed to make an enemy of the boss – the most feared consultant in the place – and have my name forever associated with the most notorious prostitute in the north of England.

Yes, I think you *could* say I'd left my mark!

Chapter 4

The long working hours expected of nurses in the 1960s left precious little time for a social life. University students were well known for their antics, particularly during RAG Week, but that didn't extend to us. Our one day off a week and one weekend a month bordered on slave labour by today's standards. But as we were all in the same boat it didn't seem so bad at the time. There was, after all, the social hut.

This ex-nissen hut had been grudgingly set aside by the hospital board as a sort of 'hanging out' place, probably to stop us going into town and enjoying ourselves. It was of wooden construction and smelled of creosote but had a makeshift dance floor with hard chairs around the perimeter. We'd managed to steal a few comfortable ones too from the wards under cover of darkness. With Matron's permission, we were allowed to hold parties, provided there was no alcohol. It *is* amazing though, how much booze can be disguised in lemonade bottles.

If we had a party, Matron always invited the police cadets, whether we wanted them to come or not. She was clearly under the misapprehension they were pillars of the community and therefore would have a good effect on us. She was seriously mistaken in thinking them suitable companions for our innocent natures. Some were okay. Most were self-centred, full of testosterone-fuelled bravado with no conversation other than work. In short – crushing bores.

Maybe she invited them to try and make up for the ghastly post-mortem experience they had to endure. Like ourselves, the cadets were required to attend at least one during their training. They frequently fainted. It was an emasculating experience when it happened in front of us sweet, innocent, fragile females – particularly when we laughed at them.

And there was the mortuary technician. If anyone was ever born to do a job, it was 'Mad' Mick Maloney. He possessed a deep, ogre-like roar of a laugh that seemed impossible to come from his ashen, cadaverous face. He smelled of embalming fluid, and just to complete the picture, had a withered hand and a pronounced limp. It was the legacy of suffering from polio as a child. Mick needed no make-up on Halloween. He could have worked for Hammer horror films earning millions instead of the pittance the NHS paid him. But Mick loved his work and took great pride in it.

I suppose it takes all sorts.

When you crept past the Ivy Cottage – and that was the only way to get to the nurses' home – his laugh would boom out from inside, sending you scuttling for cover. One couldn't imagine what was going on behind the door that was so funny. You'd be hard-pressed to find any member of the medical profession who calls their home Ivy Cottage.

If Mick heard someone passing by, he'd pop his head out and say, 'Coming in for a cuppa, luv?' His solemn expression never changed.

No bloody fear! There was something terribly sinister about his brown janitor's coat, stained with what, one could only imagine.

Ivy Cottage was indeed cloaked in ivy. Its tendrils clawed at the door and the tiny opaque window like grasping bony fingers. It was dark except for a single candle, lit whenever a body had been laid out in preparation for relatives to view, as if to herald that someone was in.

It fell to the second-year nurse working on Bamford Ward to accompany those relatives. That was me and I hated it. Mick Maloney would meet me at the door, solemn-faced, a clean coat donned for the occasion. Throughout the viewing, he stood with his back against the wall looking straight ahead like a temple guardian.

Today however, he'd come to the ward to collect me. I suppressed a shudder, more at the sight of him with his slow lumbering gait than the forthcoming task.

'I just thought I'd come and warn thee, lass,' he began in his familiar doom-laden tone. 'It's a kiddie!'

'Oh, no!' I sighed deeply.

'No more than four from that motorway pile-up a couple o'weeks back. He was killed outright – broke his neck.'

'I know,' I said sadly. 'I was there.'

'Oh 'ell! That must've been grim. Well come and see him first and it won't be such a shock for thee.' The shock had been and gone the night I took him from a weeping fireman and wrapped his still-warm little body in a blanket, but I appreciated the thought. Mick was trying to prevent me wailing whilst the parents did just that. Some chance!

'His mum and dad were outside the mortuary last week,' I said as we walked outside. 'I was coming to the porters' lodge to find you but when I got back, they'd gone.'

He stopped walking. 'No, you didn't, lass.'

I stopped too. 'No, I didn't, what?'

'You didn't see his mum and dad. Not outside the mortuary, you didn't.'

'Yes, I did, Mick. They were really distressed – well his mum was. I didn't see his dad's face clearly. She asked me if I'd seen her boy, Joshua. That's his name, isn't it? It didn't register at the time; it was the child from the accident.'

Mick stared at me, a strange look on his face. 'Yes,' he said. 'Joshua Frazer. But that couldn't have been his mother and–'

'But it was,' I interrupted again. 'She said–'

'Nurse!' he said firmly. 'You couldn't have. And how do I know that? I know that because his father died shortly after the accident – and he's in there.' He pointed to Ivy Cottage. 'As for the mother, she was unconscious on the intensive care unit until two days ago. And she's only just fit enough now to identify them both. You *must* have been mistaken!'

We reached the entrance with its solitary candle burning in the window and I followed Mick into the dimly-lit room. Shadows danced on the walls as hot wax dripped filigree patterns onto the sill.

The small child lay on the table, his head supported by a velvet-covered plinth, his small hands carefully clasped round a bunch of fresh daisies. His eyes were closed, and he looked like a sleeping angel. I choked back emotion, my cheeks hot in the otherwise cool room. It was such an inappropriate place for a little child, there amongst the old who'd lived their lives. Not a place for a sweet, innocent boy taken before his time. That morning the family had set off on a day out or whatever menial thing they had to do with no way of knowing this was the end. Nothing would ever be the same again. The family had been cut in two, the woman left alone with a baby.

With my thumb, I brushed a stray curl from his cold forehead, stroking his brow gently. It's a gesture all women possess by instinct – the need to protect, cherish and comfort. It was some sort of catalyst and I sobbed on Mick's shoulder, soaking his rough janitor's coat, not caring what he smelled of or how sinister he seemed. His act of kindness had done me a huge favour. It was selfless and caring, and from that moment I saw him in a very different light.

'Blow your nose, lass.' He passed me a handkerchief. 'We've a job to do. I'll go and fetch the mother. Are you ready now?'

I nodded. 'We're only ever allowed to borrow them for a while, aren't we?' I asked sadly as he walked slowly towards the door. 'And Mick?'

He turned

'Thank you.'

I stood alone with my thoughts until the woman walked haltingly in, as if afraid to wake the sleeping child. Slowly, she crossed to him and placed her face next to his, cradling his body in her arms and rocking him the way she'd done so often. We withdrew to the ante-room to allow her to spend time alone with her son. 'It's her!' I whispered. 'It's the woman I saw outside here more than a week ago.'

Mick didn't reply, merely blowing out a long, slow breath. After a few minutes, he turned to face me. 'Okay lass. I believe you, but you haven't half given me the creeps!'

'Don't tell me...' I began, 'that you work in here day and night alone with dead people and you've never seen or heard anything you can't explain.'

He sniffed. 'Look, Nurse, it's the living you have to worry about – and no, I haven't.' He quickly looked away.

I gave him a sideways glance and raised my eyebrows because I knew that 'Mad' Mick Maloney was lying.

She joined us in the ante-room, this frail woman only just beginning to recover from her own physical injuries. She'd lost her family in a split second of horror that was not her doing and she was broken. The mental scars would not heal so easily.

'I'll take you to where you're being picked up,' I said. 'Are you comfortable enough to get there?' She nodded, and we walked. She held on tightly to my arm, head bowed, tears running silently down her cheeks.

I looked straight ahead watching the happy, smiling little boy carried aloft by his father only a few yards ahead of us. He placed him down and they both turned to wave to his mother. It was a child-like wave. He blew baby kisses as together they walked into the distance, hand in hand.

How I wished his mother could have seen what I saw. It would surely have brought comfort to her – but I knew it wasn't the right time. I took a deep breath and said nothing.

Chapter 5

With the end of the second year of training fast approaching, much more was expected of us. Next year things would be *very* different. We'd be given increasing responsibility and expected to work on our own initiative – though supervised by a trained nurse. We were also expected to behave in accordance with that responsibility, on or off duty.

'No carousing around town bringing the hospital into disrepute!' as Matron put it. And Matron was a fearsome character – unmarried. They all were. Like nuns, marriage was not a consideration in those days. They were wedded to the profession *and* the job. Men didn't figure at all. Ours was the stereotype on which all the others were fashioned.

Miss Olivia Ffotherington – with two f's – had been a debutante who, after her London season, was expected to secure a catch worthy of her family's social status. That was a man suitable to continue the bloodline of the Berkshire Ffotheringtons by producing at least an heir and a spare. Any money was therefore retained within the family of landed gentleman farmers.

There was just one teensy-weensy problem. Olivia grew from a plain child into the ugliest young woman anyone had ever seen. Short of a rich, blind suitor coming forward at the last-minute, her marriage prospects seemed desperately poor. When all attempts at matchmaking came to nothing, there remained two choices. It was either the church or the nursing profession. Olivia chose the latter, turning her back on her family and sensibly leaving the breeding to someone else.

Young Olivia found her niche, steadily climbing the ranks of the nursing hierarchy. In the 1940s she settled in Derbyshire at our hospital, rapidly becoming known as a strict disciplinarian especially where her nurses were concerned.

On the children's ward, she was known as 'the child frightener', sending small patients scurrying to hide under the bedclothes whenever she appeared to do a ward round. Shelagh – who always called a spade a spade – remarked on more than one occasion that if *she* had a nose that big, she'd have sought help from the surgeons long ago! There was no arguing. It *was* on the larger side of huge. She had a 'north eye', where one eyeball gravitated upwards while the other stayed where nature intended it to be.

Poor woman! Definitely someone you'd have only wanted to meet in full daylight. Obviously, she'd accepted long ago that her features were unable to be improved and decided to level the playing field. Hence the imposition of the 'no make-up' rule!

Some things are obvious when working with patients. Jewellery might damage fragile skin when moving and handling. Long nails may scratch and chipped nail varnish harbours germs. Loose bits and pieces worn in the hair tend to drop off and may find their way into some poor soul's body cavity. Long hair flaps around and is annoying.

All the above was both understandable and sensible. But where was the harm in a bit of powder and paint to enhance our appearances? After all, we all looked the same in our regulation uniforms, caps and aprons. What possible hazard could a smear of lipstick and a bit of eye shadow present?

Well, everything, according to Miss Ffotherington – 'Ffothers' behind her back. She was also in the habit of policing the length of our uniform dresses. If you passed her in the corridor, she'd nod curtly and you were expected to reply with a polite 'Good morning/evening, Matron', resisting the urge to curtsey though I'm sure she considered you to be in the presence of royalty. She would suddenly shout, 'Nurse…kneel!' If the hem of your dress didn't reach the floor, you were immediately sent to the sewing room to get it lengthened. We wore different coloured petersham belts to denote our year of training. If you pulled it tight enough, it was possible to hitch up the dress a couple of inches, so it didn't look *quite* so much like a ballgown. This was the late 1960s and we liked to look our best. It was the trendy era after the austerity of the war years with its rationing. It was the time of pale pancake make-up, white Twiggy-style lipstick and kohl-framed black eyes with lashings of mascara that came in a small cake you had to spit on and apply with a brush.

Matron would have none of it. We were to appear 'au naturel' and she'd be constantly on the prowl to check compliance. And that was not all she patrolled.

Behind every ward kitchen door was a metal bin with a lid – the pig bin. She'd check each one daily to ensure food wasn't being wasted. In other words, could we save money by not feeding the pigs too well? A local farmer collected the swill twice a week and I wouldn't be surprised if Matron benefited with the odd chop and a couple of pounds of sausages on a regular basis.

By the end of the 60s, tights were becoming readily available and cheap. What an innovation! No longer did we have to put up with those uncomfortable suspender belts, even if they *did* figure prominently in the dreams of a lot of men. Gone was the cold zone of exposed flesh between the stocking top and the knickers' line that always showed under a tight skirt. Though, undoubtedly less sexy, tights were a godsend. But Matron managed to make even those boring. They had to be all the same shade, the ubiquitous American tan. Why any American should have a tan *that* colour I don't know. It was a pale corn/taupe 'nothing' colour, but at least the ladders didn't show too much.

Our shoes had to be sensible, black and laced. How can nurses' uniforms ever be the stuff of fantasy? A *less* sexy look would have been hard to find. I suspect it's the intimate things we do for our patients, because the whole idea of the ensemble was designed to be starched and formal. The moment you put it on, your role was clearly defined, and you knew who you were and what was expected of you.

In the days of the cap and apron, you felt the part – unlike today. The dresses and tunics we wear now were – allegedly – the product of a top design team. It's been suggested they were either drunk or on something at the time. Or by someone more suited to designing tall, impossibly thin buildings with no bulging bits. Unfortunately, *we* come in all shapes and sizes, from the anorexically skinny to those of more generous proportions. If those designers had done the job properly we'd feel good in them. That isn't the case. All the accessories have been dispensed with; hospital qualification badges that were worn with so much pride;

caps, aprons, scissors and frilly cuffs – all gone under the banner of health and safety. With all possible infection risks removed, I've yet to find anyone who's been maimed by the wearing of a hospital badge. Perhaps it's so we won't be tempted to use it as a weapon to jab troublesome patients.'

For forty years' service the management proudly presented me with a blue enamelled pin with a big 40 on it. I smiled and shook hands graciously. It's a good job the CEO couldn't read minds.

What use is this bloody thing? You won't allow me to wear it! Oh, progress! What a lot you've got to answer for.

During *our* training, Matron invented the health and safety rules as she saw fit. No running – except in the case of major haemorrhage. No eating on duty – except in the staff dining room – a sackable offence if you were caught. And in bed by ten with one late pass per week until eleven, provided you'd earned it. So, by way of keeping us from getting restless and mutinying, she persuaded the consultants to give the odd party in the social hut. This one was to mark the end of our second year of training for those who'd survived those first two, fun-filled years.

There had been twenty of us to begin with and we'd lost six along the way. Two transferred their studies to other hospitals. One had a nervous breakdown whilst working on Casualty after incurring the wrath of Sir Ivor, and Jane Lord ran off to Gretna Green with her secret fiancé and got married. She'd been required to leave, as such shocking behaviour wasn't allowed. Even the very plausible Marjorie Allen couldn't have stretched out her pregnancy for another year and a bit, without anyone noticing. And there was Beth Emmanuel who'd run off with one of the junior doctors and been sacked in her absence.

Matron took no prisoners when it came to the rules, so the party had come as a pleasant surprise. It was a rare opportunity to cast aside the starched uniform and dress outrageously under the noses of the nursing hierarchy. But I couldn't have cared less whether I went or not.

'Oh, come on, Pao,' said Shelagh the night before, as we sat in my room. 'It'll–'

'Do *not* tell me it'll do me good!' I rounded on her.

'I know it's only a short time since...'

'Robbie's death,' I said firmly. 'Four months, two weeks and five days and it's all right, Shelagh. You *can* say his name.' She shook her head – a helpless gesture of frustration.

'I know there's not a day goes by when you don't think of him at least a dozen times,' she said, gently placing her hand on my arm, 'probably wishing you'd said this or that.'

I nodded. There were times I wished I'd never met him and then it wouldn't hurt so much. There were deep emotions I wasn't ready to share with anyone yet – not even Shelagh. 'I'm sorry, Shelagh,' I said. 'I know you mean well but I just can't face it yet.'

She stood, hands on hips. 'Oh, I'm not going to put up with this nonsense anymore. You can get yourself dressed and ready to go by 7pm because I'm coming to get you. If you think I'm going by meself, then you're mistaken, so yer are. Now, get yer feckin' act together, will yer?'

I sighed.

'And,' she went on, 'I'm not missing it for the world. Have yer seen the new intake of anaesthetists? There's one–'

'Okay, enough!' I held up my hands in submission. 'I'll come, if only to save you from yourself.'

'That's my girl!' She tossed her hair back and turned to leave.

I smiled at her disappearing rear and shook my head. She knew a thing or two about psychology did Shelagh.

Judging by the time it took me to get ready for the party, anyone would have thought I'd a wardrobe full of clothes to choose from. I tried every single outfit, only to return it to its hanger with a grunt. In frustration, I took down the mirror from the wall to get a full-length view of myself. As I posed between changes in my skimpy underwear, it was obvious how much weight I'd lost these past months.

Small wonder nothing fits!

Despairing of finding *anything* to wear, I eventually settled on a black and white miniskirt with matching top I'd picked up in the Kings Road on one of our girlie jaunts the previous year. The skirt could be spun round if I breathed in *and* it was only a size six. Hurriedly, I tucked the top into the waistband and added a broad black PVC belt and high laced white boots with heels. Then after pinning up my hair, put on make-up for the first time in months. With the mascara brush poised, I heard a soft rustling behind me like wind through ripening corn. Tilting my chin to sniff the air, I thought I caught a suggestion of Blue Grass perfume.

'Linnie?' I whispered cautiously. 'Linnie...I do so hope it's you.' I stood still for a moment to wonder if I'd imagined the scent that always came with my friend and spirit guide. After Robbie died, it seems they'd all deserted me like rats leaving a sinking ship – and I *had* been sinking! For the first time in my life, I was truly alone. The voices had left me and no amount of begging or pleading made them return.

The air was unnaturally still, and I lay on the bed and began to breathe slowly. In...out...in, and with each breath, I fell deeper into the warmth and comfort of a purple mist. It softened, swirled and whispered my name. Linnie's soft features materialised in front of me, her hair flying as she spun round me slowly. 'Linnie, please stay with me.' She stopped, her face now bathed in soft, ethereal light as she spoke.

'You know I can't. You need me less and less.'

'I need you now. Don't go...please! I still need you.'

'You'll find your own way out of this,' she whispered in my ear. 'He's gone – but he hasn't gone. He can't because you won't allow him to. You must let him go, Pao. Your love is a prison stronger than any with bars and locks. Set him free.'

'I can't, Linnie. Not yet.'

'Yes, you can. You must, because it's time for you yourself to move on and it's time for *me* to do that too.'

'You're not leaving me as well, Linnie? I don't want you to leave me.'

'I'll never leave you. I told you that but want and need are very different things. I'll not be far away. Now let go of his hand, Paola and find another.'

'No!'

'You will. One day soon you will!' And with a rush of air like a speeding train, she was gone.

There was a loud knock, the door opened and Shelagh's head appeared. 'What *are* you doing? This is no time to sleep, and *what* is that smell? It's like old ladies' scent. Tell me you're not wearing that, Pao.'

'Don't worry,' I said, patting down my hair. It was just an old friend who called in. Let's go, shall we?'

Shelagh looked around the room, then at me, and raised her eyes to heaven.

The disco was in full swing. 'Boomer' Pashley had brought along his sound equipment. Or what was left of it after Shelagh landed on it during the pantomime rehearsal the previous year. *And* there was a bar!

'Bloody hell, Shelagh! The old girl must have had a turn. Either that or she's reformed. She won't come, will she? I bet she's got her spies out though to make sure we don't drink too much.'

'Well,' said Shelagh with a wicked grin, 'let's give them something worthwhile to report back.' She seized my hand and we headed for the bar. 'Two ridiculously large, double gin and tonics please – and you can forget the ice and lemon, darling. Just top them up with more gin.'

It was amazing. Get rid of the uniforms and we all looked normal. We had legs on show – some longer than others – and we had grown further inches in our stilettos. Not that most of us could walk far in them. Transformed, we could laugh loudly, scream if we wanted without fear of reprisals and flirt shamelessly with anything in trousers. That's what the simple act of divesting a uniform gave us – freedom!

After tipping down her oversized gin and tonic, Shelagh succeeded in wrapping herself around the new anaesthetist who'd been propping up the bar, drinking his pint and minding his own business. We were all equal now and there was an unwritten rule that said, 'whatever happens in the hut stays in the hut'.

I sipped my drink and, with a sharp pang in the pit of my stomach, watched the couples dancing. It had been a while since I'd danced with someone like that: bodies touching, strong arms around me, a warmth that was irreplaceable. Boomer then made it ten times worse by putting on a slow, smoochie record. In a moment of panic, I headed for the bar to drown my sorrows. It wasn't that I didn't want to dance, but just hadn't the heart – not yet. It was too soon and enjoying myself still felt like a betrayal of Robbie's memory.

The doors were opened to let in air. The nights were getting lighter and summer would soon be approaching. It'd been a cold and lonely winter which seemed to last forever.

The consultants had come to the party, casually dressed for once, except Jonathan Lockley who was in a suit and bow tie. I'm sure he never took the damn thing off, not even in bed. I couldn't imagine anyone who would have been able to verify it as Lockley was the most disagreeable little man on the planet.

'Oh, Pao…he's hot!' exclaimed Shelagh as she joined me at the bar.

'Who…Lockley?' I asked with disgust. She grimaced. 'Oh, your gas man.'

'He's an absolute gentleman and very reserved.' For a second she looked disappointed, then brightened. 'Never mind we'll soon change that. I fully intend to snog him senseless before the night's out. Let's see how much of a gentleman he is when he's had the taste of a *real* Irish woman.'

I thought he looked a bit *too* reserved. It was his eyes. There was just… Shelagh saw my expression. 'What?'

'I was just thinking he might be gay.'

She shot me a look of panic. 'Oh no, you don't think so, surely? Well my friend, if that's the case, I'm going to make it my mission to turn him around. *That* is too good to go to waste. Watch me and weep, Pao.'

I laughed. 'Hey, look who's over there.' The unmistakable form of Sir Ivor sat in the corner on his own.

'Look here, I'll make you a bet,' said Shelagh, mischief in her eyes. She liked the odd wager.

'What?' I asked, folding my arms.

'I'll give you ten shillings if you can get the old man to dance.'

'Are you crazy? He already thinks I stand under a red lamp in my spare time, without propositioning him further, don't you think?'

'All right,' said Shelagh, 'a pound. Now think how many pairs of tights you can buy with that.'

'A pound?' I said considering the possible transaction. I was tempted. Not by the prospect of financial reward but emboldened by the large amount of gin I'd drunk. 'Okay then,' I said, inclining my head towards the new anaesthetist. 'You're on, but if your new beau does turn out to swing the other way, you owe *me* another pound.'

'Done,' said Shelagh, shaking my hand vigorously. 'But just remember that if neither come off, *you* owe *me* two pounds.'

I drained my glass and set it on the bar. The barman raised his eyebrows.

'Another? By 'ell, you two know how to put it away.'

'Just fill it up because I may need another drink in a few minutes.' And smoothing down my skirt, tottered over in my high-heeled boots to where Sir Ivor sat with a half-pint of beer that looked lost in his huge fist. He was so flattened against the wall, he seemed to be wearing the curtains. Standing in front of him, I gave an inane smile.

'Good evening, Sir Ivor. Are you enjoying yourself?'

From his deadpan expression it was difficult to tell whether his was or not.

'Ah, my little lap pet, you are transformed somewhat.' I made to smile. 'Into what, I'm not so sure, but a little improvement nevertheless.'

The smile died on my lips. Couldn't he have been more appreciative of the time it took me to get ready? Gosh, he certainly knew how to treat a woman!

He pointed to my skirt. 'And pray tell, what *is* that you're only just wearing?'

'It's a miniskirt, Sir Ivor.'

'Ah, a *miniskirt*. And I see you have legs – quite nice legs, as a matter of fact. I hope you are wearing suitable underwear. I'd hate you to catch cold.'

I flushed a deep shade of crimson, embarrassed. Did he *really* need to comment on my dress sense and I couldn't believe he was asking about my underwear! 'Would you like to dance, Sir Ivor?'

'Dance?' He considered the question for a few seconds. 'Dance?' he repeated, finger and thumb massaging his chin as if weighing up the odds. He looked at me. 'Sorry, Nurse, I can't dance.'

'I could teach you,' I offered meekly.

He guffawed loudly. 'Oh, I'm sure there's *a lot* of things you could teach me my little lap pet, but be assured that dancing will not be one of them.'

'But it's easy,' I said. 'You just stand there and–'

'No,' he said holding up his hand like a policeman stopping a bus. 'I *don't* dance.'

I wasn't giving up. There was a pound at stake, so I folded my arms and tapped my foot – not unlike Tissie, no longer in awe of him. We were not at work now. 'Why ever not?'

He sighed patiently. 'If you insist?' Slowly, as if to a small child, he stood and whispered in my ear. 'Because when I dance, I sweat. And when I sweat, my balls itch – and when that happens, I *can't* dance! See?'

There really was no answer to that. The vision of him scratching at his sweaty undercarriage was not one I'd care to replay. I quickly muttered something ridiculous like, 'Have a nice evening then' and, sloping back across the dance floor, drank another large gin, straight down. From time to time, I glanced his way thinking he didn't look well.

I *was* determined to dance at this party and my partner came in the guise of 'Mad' Mick Maloney who I hardly recognised. He wore a suit with a rounded collar like those the Beatles favoured, and for once he didn't smell like one of his charges. He'd been liberal with the Old Spice aftershave as well!

I couldn't refuse when he asked me, not after the massive rebuff I'd just had. We bopped away happily for a few records until Boomer Pashley saw fit to put on another slow one, so I made my excuses and headed for the loo. Despite Mick's recently enhanced reputation in my eyes *and* his new appearance, I'd still no compulsion to make intimate bodily contact with him.

In the toilets, Shelagh stood beside me in front of the mirror backcombing her hair. 'Hey, Pao! It's not a bad do is this? I'm glad Matron didn't turn up though.'

'I expect she'll be tucked up in bed with a mug of Horlicks by now,' I said. 'But you can bet your life her spies will be reporting back first thing in the morning.' I dried my hands. 'Did you have any luck with the new anaesthetist?'

'Did *you* have any luck with Sir Ivor?' she countered.

'You first!' I put on another layer of lipstick.

'Why?'

'Because I asked first. Don't be so pedantic.'

Shelagh gave in. 'No, but it wasn't for the want of trying! I'm sure you're right, Pao. Probably gay as a new spring lamb.' She sighed. 'What a waste of a fabulous hunk of manhood. That's a pound I owe you.'

'No, that makes us quits. Sir Ivor wouldn't dance with me either.'

'That's a shame, so it is.' Simultaneously, we re-applied our mascara.

'Hi, I'm James. Can I buy you a drink?'

I hadn't noticed his approach due to the loud music. I'd been trying to side-step the attentions of Mick who, having found a partner at last, wasn't about to let go so easily. The last dance with its possibility of a snog was rapidly slipping away from him. The deep, though pleasant voice came from Shelagh's well-chased anaesthetist – and he *was* good looking.

'Thank you,' I nodded and smiled. 'I'd love one, but only lemonade.' *Because I've had far too much gin already.* 'My name's Paola, by the way.'

His face broke into an amazing smile which set his blue eyes twinkling. 'Yes, I know. Don't go anywhere.'

He returned with drinks and we sat at a small table.

'How are you settling in?' I asked, unsure how to break the ice. I hadn't been in this situation with a man since…

'Dance with me?' He interrupted the flow of hurt that had begun to rise again.

We danced the 'Hippy shake' and the 'Twist' and suddenly it was time for the last dance. As the strains of 'A Whiter Shade of Pale' by Procol Harum began, I'd the urge to run, far away to a safe place where couples weren't holding each other. In desperation, I looked round for Shelagh. Then, James pulled me close, his arms going around me. For a second, I froze. The last time I… I closed my eyes hardly daring to breathe. My arms went around his neck, my cheek against the soft wool of his sweater as he held me firmly. My mind raced as we danced towards midnight. *It's only a dance, for God's sake! No, it's not – it never will be again. So, what are you going to do? Shut yourself away? Or go into a convent, perhaps?*

I relaxed in his arms and he began to nuzzle my neck and ear lobe, his soft hair brushing my face. The lights in the room dimmed and as the music ended his lips found mine, gently at first then with an urgency of desire. He pulled me closer, our bodies touching, enfolding me like a soft cloak and awakening something I thought was gone forever.

The music faded, and the lights went up. Couples were breaking apart, some a little embarrassed and bidding each other 'Good night'. But he still held me close.

'Paola Green...you're beautiful,' he whispered in my ear.

'So are you,' I whispered back, unable to drag my eyes from his soft blue ones, the colour of forget-me-nots.

He smiled. 'Can I see you again, pretty lady?'

'I expect we'll see quite a lot of each other around here,' I said as we finally broke apart.

'You know very well what I mean.'

My answer was an enigmatic smile to rival that of the Mona Lisa. Over his shoulder, I saw Shelagh leaning against the wall, her arms folded and a pseudo-reproachful look on her face. I shrugged.

Later as we walked – or tottered – back to the nurses' home a bit the worse for gin, we held onto each other for support.

'Paola Green, you're a thief. A thief *and* a brazen scoundrel,' retorted Shelagh, though not nearly as miffed as she sounded. 'Trying me best all night, so I was. And *you* come along and pinch him from underneath me very nose.' There were shrieks of laughter from us as we reached the door. 'Well?' she demanded. 'What was he like, yer shameless hussy?'

'*Definitely* not gay!' I cried, as we burst into another fit of laughter.

Shelagh grinned. 'So, that's a quid *you* owe *me*.'

I shook my head slowly and smiled at her innocently. 'And worth every flaming penny.'

Chapter 6

Cass Ferrino had been careful to spare us none of the gory details as she leaned forward with a look of conspiracy on her face. Her eyes narrowed.

After all, it was easy to discuss cold-blooded murder in the warmth and safety of the Co-op café on a late Saturday afternoon. Therese Donet, Mary Delaney, Shelagh and I were all silent throughout the telling, our heads bowed close together as if plotting some gross political act of terror.

There was only one topic of conversation in our town. The body of a young hitch-hiker had been found in woods just off Junction 29 of the M1 motorway. She'd been beaten, raped and strangled with a length of electric flex before being dumped in a copse of trees alongside the motorway. It explained the number of police vehicles with sirens blaring around town the previous night. The hourly bulletins on the local radio station reported that no one had yet been arrested.

The young woman's name was Barbara Mayo and she'd remain in our collective consciousness for many years, as her murderer has never been caught. Cass had been going out with a young police constable and working with me on Bamford Ward. She'd also drawn the short straw and accompanied the relatives when it came to identification.

It'd been a harrowing task, but much more so when private grief is conducted in the public eye. From country-wide the press descended on the town and every Tom, Dick and Harry, including a BBC outside broadcast unit, had taken up residence in our hospital car park. Both police and hospital management had briefed all members of staff *not* to discuss the murder with anyone – even close friends and family. And especially with colleagues, which is exactly what they did!

Cass had been moved, though not fazed by the state of the once-beautiful young woman whose life had been so brutally cut short. She'd regaled us with the details including the ligature marks around her neck and how she'd been kicked both before and after death.

Apart from a few grimaces, we were not easily shocked these days. Maybe a couple of years ago, but not now. We were third-year student nurses, and looking back, it's disturbing how quickly we'd become de-sensitised to the horrors inflicted on people. No less was expected of us, for what use is a gibbering wreck to anyone? Feelings come later after you've gone home and closed the door behind you.

Even so, when Cass finished her tale, a collective shudder went around the table and with no wish to hang around, we drained our frothy coffees and scraping back the chairs, prepared to go our separate ways.

'See you back at the home, Pao,' said Shelagh. 'I'm just nipping to Littlewoods to buy some new tights. Some bugger's nicked mine off the radiator again!' She glanced out of the window. 'Oh hell, it's chucking down, so it is. It rains more here than back at home. Bloody weather!' she exclaimed, pulling up the collar of her coat.

'Oh, is that the time?' I asked looking at the café clock. 'I'd come with you, but I've got an evening lecture and we've been talking far too long.'

'A lecture? On a Saturday?' they asked in unison.

'It's a special. They're coming over from Sheffield School of Midwifery.'

'Well that's something *I* certainly won't be doing,' said Cass with a distasteful curl of her lip. 'Just imagine spending your entire working life between women's legs. God, it's a man's dream but it's not for *this* woman!' We all laughed and on that lighter note, headed for home.

'Watch out for the murderer, Pao,' called Mary Delaney as I walked away.

'Oh, get away with you,' I said. 'He'll be long gone.'

Darkness was falling, leaving that funny sort of ethereal twilight you get as autumn changes to winter. There was a chill in the air, a hint of frost to come before much longer. I wrapped my scarf tightly around my neck and picked up my wicker shopping basket and grimaced as the wind whipped around the corner of the Co-op.

With hindsight – which is a wonderful thing – the decision to take a short cut along Union Walk was not a very bright one in the circumstances. However, the prospect of walking much further in the rain was not appealing. The narrow passage with high brick walls on either side was about five hundred yards long and connected two areas of town. Lit by the occasional street lamp, it was still quite dark. Fumbling in my pocket for a torch, I set off humming 'Tears of a Clown' by Smoky Robinson and the Miracles.

As I reached halfway, I thought I heard footsteps behind me and a quick backward glance told me I was right. A tall man in a dark overcoat was following some distance away. He too wore a long scarf wound round his neck and lower face. I hummed louder and quickened my step, clutching the basket tighter and mouthing the words of the song. 'Don't let my sad expression give you the wrong impression…. Oh, baby I know…' Suddenly the torch battery failed and the footsteps behind me were getting louder and closer. My chest tightened, and I began to run. The man also began to run, his steps keeping pace with my own.

It's Barbara Mayo's murderer and now he's after me. I'm going to be horribly done in! No one will find me until tomorrow and my family must live out their days in the public eye. An image of them sitting at the press conference weeping flashed before my eyes.

'Well, bugger that!' I said aloud finding backbone from somewhere and, stopping dead in my tracks, turned and prepared to fight for my life. I raised the torch in readiness.

My 'assailant' stopped a couple of feet from me and bent forward, hands on knees, breathing hard.

'I'm sorry,' he gasped. 'I didn't mean to frighten you.'

I was not so easily fooled and raised the torch higher ready to bring it down hard on his head.

He shrieked in alarm. 'Don't hit me…*please* don't hit me!'

'Why the hell are you following me?' I yelled, still brandishing the torch. 'You…you idiot! Well?' I demanded.

47

'What do you want?'

The man cowered pathetically, unconvinced I wasn't about to club him to death. 'I'm sorry...so sorry,' he bleated. 'You see, my toupee blew off on the Co-op corner and...I'm afraid it's in your shopping basket.'

I stared in disbelief at what looked like the remains of a dead hamster lying on top of my shopping. Gingerly, I picked it up between finger and thumb and passed it to him at arm's length.

He backed away, seemingly still uncertain whether I was going to hit him.

Back in the safety of the nurses' home, I thought of the trusting young woman who'd travelled alone. She may have accepted a lift from a seemingly innocent-looking stranger. It was a small error of judgement that cost her life.

I vowed never to use that short cut again.

Chapter 7

Christmas came and went and before we knew it was early March, and the final year of our training. We'd grown up – all of us – from the rather silly young women who'd been thrown together from different cultures and backgrounds. We'd blossomed into adulthood, made wiser than our years by the daily trials of the nursing profession, and hardened against tragedy while caring for all who needed it. I'd loved every moment of the journey so far. That comfort comes from knowing you've found your niche.

Bamford was a male surgical ward, tacked on like an after-thought to the main hospital buildings. After the war, the need for male surgical wards increased a great deal. Battlefield wounds still needed attention years later. Like our social hut, it was made of creosoted timber and wouldn't have looked out of place on a military base. Despite the advantage of providing thirty more beds, it had its disadvantages too. It stood alone, a good way from the main hospital so when anyone went to theatre they had to go outside. Wheeled on a trolley across an open yard at the mercy of the elements was far from ideal. We tried to make the journey as smooth as possible. But whenever it rained or snowed, the process took on the appearance of something out of a 'Carry On' film. With the patient on the trolley, often with drips and drains, they'd also have to be covered with blankets to stop them freezing. On top was placed a huge brown rubber sheet to keep the rain off. And all this after major surgery. It was amazing anyone survived!

That was not the end! When the planners had designed Bamford Ward, space was at a premium and it had to be squeezed in between other buildings. This unfortunately lay at the bottom of quite a steep incline. So, not only had we the patient, catheter bags, drips, drains and a large umbrella to contend with, but the added problem of controlling a trolley with no brakes down a steep hill. It was more by luck that the poor chap got there in one piece at all.

Someone had to hold back the weight of the trolley to prevent it careering away – and that someone was Brian, the theatre porter who was only five feet five inches tall himself. At least he was well anchored, having size thirteen feet, about the size of two small canoes. This was fortunate because at the other end was some poor little student nurse. Brian was not known for his cheery persona and cussed each time we approached the slope. In winter it resembled the Cresta Run with no one having had the presence of mind to grit it.

Today, that was all a bad memory. Spring was in the air and though not exactly balmy just yet, there were fluffy white fair-weather clouds littered across a clear blue sky. I all but skipped up the path to Bamford Ward from the nurses' home, but it *was* theatre day and there would be many trolleys to push up and down the incline before the shift ended. I hoped Brian would be in a good mood, though we two *did* have an unfortunate history. If it had happened today, I'd surely have been dragged before the nursing disciplinary council and poor Brian taken out, tied to a post and shot.

It happened the previous winter – one of the longest anyone could remember. Snow fell onto frozen snow, then more on top of that. I'd been drafted in to do a short stint on the male medical ward as we were right in the middle of a 'flu epidemic. Those staff still standing were moved around the wards to provide some sort of daily cover. Unfortunately, the germs didn't stop at the doors of the porters' lodge either and there wasn't anyone left to shovel the snow away *or* keep the pathways clear.

Richard Bradley and I had been on a late shift with only one auxiliary nurse to help with our thirty-eight patients and we were rushed off our feet. Being on a medical ward, some of these patients were seriously ill. There was the four-bedded coronary care unit for a start. Others were stroke victims and practically helpless as well as the full gamete of conditions *not* requiring surgery.

Since 1pm we'd had four deaths, including two cardiac arrests, both with unsuccessful resuscitations despite the best efforts of the emergency team. We were doing our best, but it was barely good enough. At around 8pm Richard came to find me in the sluice room where I was emptying a stack of bedpans.

'Pao, we're stopping for five minutes. Leave all those. You and I are going to have a cup of coffee behind the kitchen door and sod the consequences. If Matron – the old mare – catches us we won't get the sack. Not unless she wants to empty those bloody things herself. Come on, babe. I've put the kettle on!'

'Oh, Richard, I love you,' I said.

He'd only been qualified a year himself and was the most overtly gay man in existence – and proud of it. Richard wore his sexuality not only on his sleeve, but on every inch of his body. And if you were still in any doubt, it disappeared the moment he spoke with an effeminate voice that matched his appearance.

'I should be so lucky,' he retorted, hand on hip. 'Now, come on. We've not had a break for the entire shift and I need a fag.'

I ignored the obvious pun and didn't need further persuading. I followed him wearily into the kitchen after a quick look up and down the corridor to make sure no one was about. Richard proffered his cigarettes.

'No thanks,' I said. 'I don't smoke.'

'You don't...' he said, surprised, 'and you in your third year?' I nodded. 'Don't worry, you soon will – everybody does! I'll give you–' The sentence was cut off by the cardiac arrest bell. I jumped, the contents of the mug spilling down my apron.

'Oh, fucking hell,' said Richard, stubbing out his cigarette. 'Not again!'

We went into action with our well-practised routine. Off came the head and foot of the bed in a few seconds as we began to administer oxygen, suction and CPR. Things had changed from the first time I did this. We no longer had to chuck the patient on the floor like a sack of potatoes. The new mattresses didn't sag and allowed us to resuscitate on the bed. With a bag and mask, we took turns at ventilation and chest compressions until the cardiac arrest team arrived, but despite their efforts, once again we lost him. Death was registered at 8.30pm.

'God forbid, Richard!' I exclaimed when everyone had left. 'What the hell have we done to deserve this lot today?' He returned the office phone to its cradle.

'Well, Pao, it's about to get a lot worse, I'm afraid. There's no night shift coming on, darlin'.'

'What?' I almost screamed.

'Every bugger's sick. They might be able to get us some relief, but it won't be till after midnight, so we're stuck with this lot, honey bunch. Now that bell can ring its ruddy 'ead off, because we're definitely having that cuppa.'

I didn't know whether to laugh or cry. 'Come on then,' I said, walking to the kitchen. 'Now shut your face and pass me a fag.'

'Shit...that didn't take long.'

'I'm going to need it.' I quickly lit the proffered cigarette and drew on it with a cough. 'Do you realise that *now* we have to lay him out as well?' If the night staff had come on at 9pm, the job would have gone to them. Now we couldn't get out of it.

We finished the task by 11pm and it hadn't been easy as he was a *very* big chap, but with our last remaining strength we managed to haul him onto the mortuary trolley. This was not the enclosed camouflaged box on wheels it is today. It was a bog-standard trolley used for transporting both the living *and* dead.

Brian was *not* a happy man. We heard him as he came huffing and chuffing up the ward long before he came into view and the grumbling got louder the closer he got. It was of course, Saturday night and we all knew what Brian liked to do on a Saturday. It was 'pop' night, and all he wanted was to get home to his bacon, egg and chips and go down to the Crown and Cushion for a few too many pints. He'd stagger home afterwards, and if he were lucky, they'd be the prospect of intimacy – no doubt involving more huffing and puffing. I couldn't dwell on that too long as Brian was not the most attractive of men. Completely bald on top, he had a comb-over that got lower and lower as time went by. The side parting was now about level with his ear and when the wind blew it lifted like a tent flap in a gale despite regular applications of sugar and water. Why do men do that? It must be uncomfortable apart from looking like something out of a circus.

Poor Brian! Apart from not being able to get home for his weekly night out and leg-over, he'd been seconded to the role of mortuary porter in Mick's absence. He looked like he hated the world and everyone in it when he arrived on the ward, wet and covered in snow.

'A right bloody carry on this is!' he complained. 'Sodding weather. Do you know what I should be doing tonight?'

'Yes, Brian,' said Richard, patiently. 'You tell us *every* Saturday.'

'Instead,' he moaned, 'I'm stuck 'ere shoving stiffs around. Tell me – is this any way for a man to earn a living? I hate that mortuary. They *know* I hate that mortuary! I mean, is it any way–'

'Brian,' I interrupted. We're all in the same boat. I don't expect he died on purpose just to do you out of your 'pop' night. Anyway, you won't get home through all this snow until–'

'If I'd wanted to transport stiffs, I'd 'ave been a bloody undertaker,' wailed Brian. 'Yer never see no bloody undertaker riding round in a Ford Anglia, do you? No! Jags and Bentleys, all of 'em!"

'Yes,' I said, losing patience. 'And usually they've got a passenger in the back. Come on, Brian, stop whingeing and I'll come and help you because it'll be icy down that slope. For God's sake, stop moaning.'

What a wonderful thing hindsight is? If only I'd gone and hidden somewhere.

We covered our passenger with the customary purple coverlet with its embroidered gold cross and set off across the ungritted forecourt. There'd been no one available to do it, though some kind soul *had* cleared a path through the snow wide enough for the trolley wheels to pass.

It had stopped snowing and the moon came out to light our way in a sky studded with myriads of stars. In some circumstances, it could have been quite romantic, except for Brian still complaining loudly. We reached the steep slope leading to the back entrance of the mortuary with its double doors away from prying eyes. There was no alternative route apart from a flight of steps to the nurses' home on the other side. Bridging the two was a low wall a few bricks high and beyond it, an area of dead space about eight feet deep. It provided a convenient area to chuck fag ends, sweet wrappers and unwanted bits of broken wheelchairs. It should have been filled in years ago and was probably on an agenda somewhere to do just that. Obviously not very near the top.

'We'd better be careful,' warned Brian. 'There's black ice 'ere. Tell you what – you take the bottom end to steady it and I'll take the top. Can't let a little lass like you take the weight, can we?'

'Very chivalrous, Brian!' I said, through gritted teeth. We always accompanied patients on their last journey. It was a final mark of respect as they left our care.

Unsteadily, we headed for the slope, the ground glassy underfoot and I clung tightly to the bar at my end of the trolley.

'I'll hold it back,' said Brian. 'Just you concentrate on keeping it straight.'

Suddenly my feet began to slide. 'Oh no, Brian, I'm slipping!' My shoes skidded first one way and then the other, the trolley following me as I hung on for dear life.

'Hold on,' cried Brian. 'Don't let go.' He fought to hold the combined weight of trolley and its cargo.

My legs zipped from under me and I fell flat on my back with a thud. 'Aaaah! I screamed more from sheer surprise than injury. Brian also screamed. Unable to hold on, he let go. The trolley passed over me, miraculously missing every limb and Brian came to rest beside where I lay.

'Oh, shit!' We yelled in unison as we watched the trolley career down the slope towards the low wall, which it hit with an almighty bump. The body gained forward momentum, shot off and disappeared into the void in a shower of snow.

Brian and I turned to each other open-mouthed, before a mixture of obscenities warmed the cold night air. Hanging on to each other, we managed to struggle to our feet and unsteadily dragged ourselves forward to peer over the wall.

Fortunately, rigor mortis was still present, but as the trolley had shed its load, the body somersaulted. All we could see in the darkness was a large pair of feet with the black-edged identification label still tied to one big toe.

'Thank goodness,' I sighed, grateful to see him all in one piece.

Brian dusted the snow from his clothes. 'Thank goodness?' he retorted loudly. 'Thank bleedin' goodness? You stupid mare. What's good about it? How the fuck do you suppose we're going to get 'im out of there, yer daft bint? I bet there's not one intact bone in his body.' His eyes were popping. 'Tell me he wasn't for a post-mortem.'

'I don't know,' I said helplessly, sensing the premature end of my nursing career fast approaching. 'Just stop complaining for once, and go for help.' I stared miserably at the upturned soles of the feet hoping it was a dream and any moment I'd wake up. But it wasn't – and I didn't.

Help came in the guise of a local mountain rescue team who, as luck would have it, were returning from a 'shout' near Sheffield. Had they not been close by, someone would have probably found me in the morning covered by a foot of snow as it was falling heavily again. I shivered despite my thick, woollen cloak.

The poor old gentleman was finally extricated from his icy tomb with a series of pulleys, with one guy having to abseil into the abyss. Our patient finally made it to Ivy Cottage two hours after he left the ward. It was the oddest rescue the team had ever done and one that could never be used as publicity for our heroes.

I thought I'd never be warm again and pneumonia would be a certainty – if Matron didn't get me first. I sat shivering in the ward kitchen looking like the abominable snowman, every digit numb, unable to feel the mug of tea Richard pressed into my hands. From the taste, it'd been laced with the medicinal brandy kept by Sister for emergencies.

To our intense relief, the night staff made it in at 3am, so Richard and I could go to our beds. It took a bit of time to finally hand over the reins to the next shift, due to multiple breaks for laughter from them. I couldn't describe the relief on reaching the nurses' home at 4am, closing the front door quietly behind me. I turned to climb the stairs and my heart sank.

Standing with arms folded and foot tapping was Tissie. Not in the mood for a wigging, I opened my mouth to get in first. Then, she smiled, for which I was unprepared.

'Nurse Green,' she said. 'Come with me. Now, you are *not* to go to bed cold. I'm surprised you didn't catch your death out there.' She beckoned me into her room. 'There's a nice hot bath prepared for you, my dear. We can't have you running the water and waking everyone, can we? I've put out soap and towels.' She closed the door behind me. I looked round, still open-mouthed.

She's got her own en-suite! I couldn't believe it – or her kindness. How she knew what had happened I'll never know. Her special radar was working overtime again. It was uncanny. I sank into the hot, bubble-laden tub and began to thaw, and when I'd finished, put on the thick white towelling robe she'd laid out for me.

As I left, I turned. 'Miss Thistlethwaite,' I began, 'thank you so–'

She held up her hands to silence me. 'Rubbish, girl. I'm merely preventing you from waking the *entire* house,' she said tersely.

I smiled and shook my head. Why is this woman, so fierce on the outside, completely incapable of accepting thanks for a kindness? 'Well, I'm very grateful anyway,' I said, reaching the door.

She merely gave a curt nod. 'And, Nurse...'

'Yes, Miss Thistlethwaite?'

'Leave Matron to me. I'll see to everything.'

I reached my room and climbed into bed to find she'd placed a couple of hot water bottles between the sheets. Robbie *had* been right when he'd said she was a wonderful person – despite the face she presented to the world.

Chapter 8

I didn't catch pneumonia and was never summoned to Matron to give an account of our escapade with the flying corpse. How Tissie did it I'll never know. Only that she was no friend of Matron, so whatever it was, probably gave her great satisfaction. She'd defended one of her girls, as she called us, and the incident was never mentioned again.

That didn't extend to the rest of the staff. Such an event was a gossiper's dream – a gift from heaven, and Paola Green was, once again, right in the middle of it. I was getting quite a reputation for all the wrong reasons and merciless teasing followed for months. Whenever I escorted a body to the mortuary, I had to endure such comments as, 'Where are you taking this one, Nurse Green? Gliding or a bit of pot-holing perhaps? Come straight back and no diversions. Okay?' I found the best way of dealing with it was not to respond and to nod and smile as though it was the first time I'd heard it, rather than the hundred and something. I hoped they'd all get fed up given time. Brian, however, was dining out on the experience for months, becoming interesting for the first time in his life.

It was with great relief when it was time for a change of scenery on nice, steady uneventful Bamford Ward, male surgical under the watchful eye of Sister Armitage. Theatre lists were on Mondays, Wednesdays and Fridays with any emergencies fitted in between. Thirty beds were arranged with military precision in two rows. There were no fixed curtains, so we had to drag screens on wheels around as required. At the far end was a sluice and treatment room that served as storage for everything else including a large oxygen cylinder that was wheeled to wherever it was needed.

Orientation for new staff often meant following someone around on a quick dash that took about two minutes. The rest was picked up along the way. Now, we have the luxury of being able to treat our student nurses and midwives as supernumerary, assigning them to a trained member of staff, teaching and holding their hands through the day's trials and tribulations. We talk them through sad and tragic situations and debrief them afterwards. This is the human face of training our students can expect today and not the 'see one, do one – now get on with it' approach of my training. We were thrown in at the deep end to sink or swim, learn or burn.

I remember being left in charge on the ear, nose and throat ward whilst the senior nurse went for her dinner. Over half the patients had been for surgery that day and I was barely six months into my nurse training. It was the middle of the night and Nurse Green was appropriately named: green as grass, wet behind the ears and a completely innocent eighteen-year-old. It's dubious I'd have even recognised the early signs of someone bleeding to death until it puddled on the floor and I slipped in it. How did I survive – and more importantly – how ever did the patients?

Wilfred Finch was sixty and a man of extremely generous proportions. The old cliché of the laughing policeman on a seaside pier came to mind as I looked at him. He'd a ruddy complexion with broken veins over his cheeks and nose that you associate with long periods working out in the open. He'd a jolly disposition, always happy and smiling, no matter what time of day or night you spoke to him. At twenty-six stone, he was extremely overweight and this was why he was on Bamford Ward awaiting surgery.

Wilfred had terrible leg ulcers that had refused to heal, despite the best attentions of the district nurses. They'd become infected and treated with several courses of antibiotics, but as the weeks went by, dead skin had accumulated around the wounds and the whole area had become very smelly. Anyone who's spent time with these patients will instantly recognise the sweet sickly odour.

'Doctors say it's all down to me weight, Nurse,' he said as I renewed the dressings.

'Well it's due to many things,' I said. 'Often poor circulation as we get older and things don't always work quite so well. Have you always been a big lad, Mr. Finch?'

He reached into his bedside locker and took out a shallow, grey stone bowl about the size of the palm of my hand. 'Oh no, lass...and please call me Wilf.'

'All right, but don't let on to Sister Armitage.' I leaned forward and whispered. 'She's a beggar for formality.'

He grinned, toothless, his eyes shining with the secret. 'Okay, Nurse Green.'

'My name's Paola.'

'Don't worry, lass. I won't tell her *that* either. Well, Paola, between you and me I've not always been fat.' He rubbed the rim of the bowl between his thumb and forefinger.

'Oh, I'm sorry, Wilf. I didn't mean to...'

He patted my hand. 'It's all right, lass, but it's summat I don't talk about very often, you see.' He rubbed the bowl's rim more vigorously.

'Sorry,' I said and quickly changed the subject. 'How long have your legs been like this?

'Oh, years,' he said.

'Well, I'm going to dress them with this special paraffin gauze. It has an antibiotic added to the sticky stuff. It'll make them much more comfortable. Then, when it's done its job we'll take you to the theatre and while you're asleep, get all the dead stuff off and leave a nice, clean area.'

'Honey,' he said, stroking the bowl with a tender touch. 'My wife used to put honey on them.'

'Honey?' I repeated.

'From my bees. Nothing's finer than honey for healing wounds. It kills bacteria, tha' knows. It used to keep me sores at bay, but since the wife died...well, I've not had t'patience to do them meself.'

'How long is it?' I asked.

He sighed. 'Three years. It's three years.' There was silence for a few minutes until he spoke again. 'Wonderful things, bees. I can sit and watch 'em coming and going all day. Everything they do has a purpose, tha' knows and they all work together for the good of t'hive and only fight back when summat interferes.'

I had a picture in my mind of this lovely man, dressed in his protective suit and veil, tending to his bees without a care in the world. 'Well,' I said, 'let's get these legs better and you'll be back with them before you know.'

His eyes locked on mine with an intensity that for a moment was frightening. 'You're so young,' he said. 'And to you the world is a very lovely place.'

Gosh, what an odd thing to say!

'Hurry up, Nurse Green and stop chattering so much. We have to get lunches out.' Sister's voice travelled the length of the ward. Wilf winked at me, the twinkle returning to his eyes.

Putting on a plastic apron over my uniform, I went to help Sister. The food smelled beautiful as always. Everything was cooked in the kitchens on site to a high standard and the chefs used fresh, local produce. Nowadays, people regard this as an innovation, but that's the way it was always done. Meals came to the ward in a heated trolley from which Sister served everyone, with us nurses acting as waitresses. We really were the Jack and Jill of all trades.

'Now, gentlemen,' she began, 'we have steak and kidney pie with peas, beans and new potatoes, or macaroni cheese. For pudding, there's cook's special apple pie and custard or Bakewell tart with ice cream. So, start thinking what you would like today.'

We made our way round the ward and came to Wilf.

'Now, Mr Finch,' said Sister. 'What would you like?' There was no answer. Wilfred looked back at her, a worried look on his face. 'Mr Finch?' Poor Wilf began to stutter hopelessly, his hands shaking.

I placed my hand gently on his shoulder sensing his confusion and discomfort. 'Shall we give you a little of each, so you don't have to choose?' I asked softly.

He looked at me, blind panic in his eyes, still unable to speak then nodded.

'Oh my God! Whatever has happened to this man?' I whispered to Sister, and carrying the plate carefully, placed it in front of him. He stared at the food as if at any moment it would jump up and bite him, and grabbing his bowl from the locker, clutched it to his chest.

Sister fixed him with a disapproving glance and moved on to

the next patient.

As soon as we were gone, Wilf grabbed his spoon and fork and began shoving food into his mouth so quickly he almost choked. Hardly able to swallow before more was forced in, his jaws moved frantically, eyes fixed on his plate. Sister and I stood at the next bed, fixated to the spot at this apparent display of gluttony. When the plate was empty, he licked it like a starving dog until not one morsel remained.

'Well!' said Sister when we were back in the ward kitchen. 'It's not difficult to see how he got to *that* size.' The performance was repeated with the pudding course and Sister was still shaking her head at tea-time. 'All I can think is that the poor man must have been starving. I want you to make sure he gets three square meals a day until his surgery. It's your responsibility Nurse Green as his nurse, but *do* try to improve his table manners a bit, will you?'

I was becoming certain that Richard was following me.

I'd worked with him on Female Medics when he'd ended up caked in gore and on the night of the famous 'flying body'. I'm sure he thought I was a jinx. Now he was doing his stint on Bamford. I loved him to bits – in a sisterly sort of way. In keeping with the outward display of his sexuality, Richard could also be very outspoken. It had gotten him into trouble on more than one occasion, and today it would land him in another heap of it.

It was the day of Wilf's operation and he'd been starved from midnight in preparation. I'd asked the night nurse to ensure he got plenty to eat before the curfew, because all my instincts told me something was very wrong *apart* from leg ulcers. He clearly had a deep-seated problem with food. It wasn't *just* that he had the manners of the pigsty. There was something very troubling behind those jolly twinkling eyes and the speed at which they changed to terror at meal times. It was the reaction of a hunted animal.

The newspaper trolley also sold sweets and chocolate and it came around the wards daily. Wilf would buy one of everything and stash them in his locker. I never saw him eat any though. He reminded me of a squirrel collecting nuts for winter. I once went in to get him a clean nightshirt and was almost killed by an avalanche of confectionary.

Richard had a theory – as he did on most things – that it was Wilf's insurance policy in case dinner didn't arrive, stating cruelly that he was just a 'fat pig'. He was a bit miffed at the way Wilf turned down all help with his personal care – the job of the male nurses – insisting on doing it himself behind the closed bathroom door. 'Doesn't seem to trust anyone, that bloke,' said Richard, striking his usual effeminate pose – bent knee, hand on hip.

I raised an eyebrow. 'Probably heard about you,' I said quietly.

'Not my type, darling,' he replied.

'I should bloody well hope not.' I was at a loss to imagine what *his* type could be – though I wasn't about to ask him.

'And he won't wear pyjamas. What's that all about? Those long-sleeved nightshirts of his – he must be roasting in here. Still, it makes it easier to do his dressings, I suppose.'

'Old men have their own little ways, Rich. Some are very private and it's not up to *us* to upset them. *You* might be like that, one day.'

He grimaced. 'But he smells, Pao, and other patients are starting to complain. I just want to give him a right good bath.'

'All humanity smells, Richard,' I said. 'Take a deep breath and get over it!'

As we wheeled Wilf into theatre, the pinched expression on his face told me he was terrified.

'It'll be all right, Wilf,' I said, my hand over his.

Suddenly, he sat bolt upright with a cry. 'My bowl…. I haven't got my bowl. I can't go without it.' He started to scramble from the trolley.

Richard tried to intervene. 'Wilf, for God's sake…it's a dish!' He was losing patience.

Wilf clutched at Richard's arm. 'It's – my – bowl!' he stammered, his eyes wide and fearful.

'Stop!' I told the porter. 'Wait a minute,' and running back to the ward retrieved the little stone dish.

He stopped panicking the second he had it clutched to his chest. Richard shot me a look that said not only was Wilf crazy, but so was I.

I glared at Richard. 'Just humour him will you and leave it to me?' Whatever this bowl represented, it was like a favourite teddy bear or a child's comfort blanket. This was an old man with a serious psychological problem and no family, and *this* was not the time to address it. The enigmatic bowl was his one source of succour.

Wilf held onto my hand tightly as we waited for the anaesthetist.

'While you're asleep, Wilf, would you like me to look after your bowl for you? I'm a bit worried it might get lost. I don't fully understand but I can see it means a lot to you,' I said.

He looked at me with those sad, empty eyes again and a tear escaped down his cheek. It was as though he'd never trusted anyone before. Then he handed me the shallow bowl. 'You'll keep it safe, Paola? It's all I have in my life.'

'But what about your home and your bees and...' I said, trying to lighten the mood.

'This *is* my life, Paola.'

'Then I'll keep it *very* safe and I promise it'll be in your hands when you wake.' Carefully, I placed it in my dress pocket and left Wilf sleeping, courtesy of my new friend, James, the anaesthetist.

While he was in the theatre, I sat looking at the little bowl made of some sort of soapstone, turning it over in my hands. It looked like an unremarkable little ashtray and I couldn't imagine why it was so special. But I knew it was. Probably only worth pennies, but it didn't matter. It was enough that it held great significance for Wilf. I was sure there was much more to this man's story and it made me profoundly uneasy, to such an extent that I made a point of going to the recovery room when Wilf woke to make sure it was the first thing he saw. I learned something that day, something I never forgot. What one person dismisses as completely insignificant may be another's world and we must tread with care.

That's how it was with Peabody's ball.

As an eighteen-year-old, I'd entered a frightening world, one I'd no previous experience of. The psycho-geriatric wards were housed in another small hospital about three hundred yards up the road from the Royal. In Victorian times, the building had been the town's workhouse where the destitute, the simple and the friendless went, kept away from public view because there was no alternative.

Workhouses were terrible places, with men separated from the women, and children from their mothers. It was a place of last resort. Many of the buildings seemed to retain an air of menace and foreboding. The old, red brick walls towered upwards as if to say, 'All here are in my shadow forever'. It was difficult when the elderly had to be brought into hospital, as many still remembered the place for what it had once been.

The nurses' dining room was a low pre-fabricated building, crouching next to one of the old blocks still used as a ward. There was an access walkway between. This ward held the disturbed that until the birth of the NHS had been called 'inmates'. Now they were 'patients', though little had changed for these people except their status on paper. The old exercise yard was fenced off from the dining room walkway.

This is where Peabody lived. No one knew whether this was his first or last name – or even how old he was for that matter. He was just Peabody. A wrinkled, little old man with a permanent stupefied grin, wearing a suit too small for him and a jumper snagged from the eight-foot, green wire fencing. He had the wide eyes of a sad spaniel and carried a soft, battered football under his arm. Peabody spent his days waiting by the fence, the fingers of one hand clutching the wide plastic mesh until he saw someone approaching. Then, with a cry of delight, his eyes lit up and he threw the ball over the fence, clapping with glee until someone retrieved it and threw it back. He was like a pet dog, never tiring of the game. This was his life, summer, winter, rain or shine. He'd be there waiting for someone – anyone – to throw back his ball, those sad eyes following your every movement until you did. In four months of working there on the Gynae ward I never heard him speak.

Then, one day, he wasn't there, just the tattered, old ball lying by the fence and no one to care. Only relief they didn't have to chase the damn thing anymore. A non-person forgotten by everyone so soon, the only thing to mark his life: an abandoned ball by the fence. It had a profound effect on me and two years later, there was Wilf. So, whatever this stone trinket was or wasn't, I was determined he should have it there in his grasp the moment he woke.

Next day, Richard and I went to check his dressings. In theatre, the surgeon had done a 'debridement'. That involved scraping away the debris to leave healthy, living skin that had a better chance of healing. Wilf was unwell and had been since returning from theatre. His temperature and pulse were raised and his blood pressure was low enough to be worrying. It was post-operative shock. Intravenous fluids were started, along with a course of strong antibiotics.

'Come on, Richard,' I said. 'While we're here, let's give Wilf a freshen up and change his nightshirt. It'll make you feel much better, Wilf.' I stroked his brow, but his eyes said nothing today as he lay holding his little bowl.

'Now then, Wilfred!' said Richard. 'Let's get you sitting up.'

There was no reply. We took his weight and leaned him forward to raise the backrest and plump his pillows. 'We're going to give you a hitch up the bed,' continued Richard, 'so give us a bit of help. Put your chin on your chest and push with your good leg. Oh, come on, Wilf man! Help us or our backs will be buggered by the time we're forty. You're a big lad, you know!'

I shot Richard a reproachful glance, as we must never say anything to make people feel inferior of humiliated. But Richard was difficult to stop once in full flow. Ignoring me, he went on. 'It's true, innit? Lifting big blokes all day long and you know what? There's no need for it.' There was no stopping him now.

'Richard...' I began.

'Absolutely no need for it at all. No fat people came out of Belsen!'

I gasped in horror at such a comment.

Wilf's eyes opened wide with shock as, looking deeply into Richard's, he slowly began to roll up the sleeve of his nightshirt. His eyes filled with tears. There on his forearm were a series of tattooed numbers. 'Oh, but they did, lad,' was all he managed to say before emotion overcame him completely.

Unable to believe what I'd just witnessed, I turned and man-handled Richard into the sluice room.

'I didn't know, Pao. How could I have known?' said Richard, genuinely upset. 'He always wears those long-sleeved shirts. Oh my God!'

'Your sodding mouth – no thought for anyone's feelings! Well, now you know *why* he wears them. What that poor man must have gone through. What he's carried with him over the years, no one can imagine. It was a *death* camp, Richard. He was in a *death* camp – and you with that gob of yours must have humiliated him beyond...' I stopped, no longer able to even look at him and I walked away slamming the door behind me. *And,* I didn't care whether any part of Richard's anatomy was caught in it or not.

Before I left after my shift, I went back to see Wilf. He lay motionless, still holding his little bowl. I placed my hand over his. There was little response as he lay with his head turned away from me. I sat silently holding his hand and closed my eyes.

The train, with its airless cattle trucks, rolled to a stop, the wheels squealing until the sliding doors were finally opened. Soldiers were lined up on the makeshift platform screaming for everyone to get out, roughly moving the old and encouraging the young with the butt of a rifle.

'Schnell. Schnell! Move quickly. Women and children to the right – men to the left!' The people stood shivering in rows as the snow fell. An officer, warmly wrapped in a woollen greatcoat walked the length of the row, swagger-stick under his arm.

'Welcome to Paradise.'

I stood behind them on the edge of the platform watching in horror, knowing my part was that of a bystander unable to change anything. I looked on as the men were marched one way and the women and children another to join 60,000 others, most of whom would die of starvation, brutality and typhus – or by being worked to death.

I moved with ease to the wire, the day the British and Americans came to liberate the camp with its walking skeletons, more dead than alive. The stench of death and decay from piles of corpses was everywhere. Help had come too late for most. They'd lain down one last time with no one left to bury them. No one to say words over them or pray for their souls.

In this hell-hole, Wilf had survived to liberation – somehow.

'Bergen-Belsen?' I whispered. It was the next night and during a quiet period, I sat with Wilf, holding his hand. He nodded and closed his eyes as if reliving the nightmare. Then, he began to talk, probably for the first time in years.

'I was captured with the rest of the battalion outside Albert in 1943 and we were marched to a village near Rheims before being transported to Germany in cattle trucks. I don't know why I was chosen, they were mainly Jews, you see. At first, we were given a little food but that soon ran out and people started to starve to death. It was unspeakable, the forced labour and the cruelty. We'd have done anything for just one morsel of rotting bread. The reason I'm alive and why I survived was because of this. He stroked the bowl as though it were a lover. The guards came with a sort of thin soup once a day, more a muddy slop of grey water really. It looked like washing up water and smelled worse, and they served it into your cupped hands. The hot liquid ran through your fingers, but I had this and could hide it in my hands. If you didn't have a container you got next to nothing.

'I often asked myself why I brought the thing with me. It's a Japanese brush bowl, something I just grabbed when we were transported. I suppose I thought it'd make a good weapon – heavy you see. I survived because of it and it was still in my hands when the British came to liberate the camp. All my mates were dead, and I was barely alive. I weighed four stone.' He paused to look at me. Tears were silently falling down my cheeks. 'Nay lass, don't you fret. I came out of that hell-hole an animal, because that's what they turned us into. That's what starvation does. It breaks your spirit and eventually it's so easy to just lie down and die. I had to learn to be a man again. I think I did.'

'You did,' I said. 'You're a very fine gentleman.' I understood now. A starving man on the very brink of death. Old habits die hard. Like a starving dog – gobble it down quickly, every scrap, in case it's taken away or somebody steals it. Store for the future – keep it safe. The fact that he'd a little bowl to drink his slop from meant he got more. It meant he survived. In the camp he'd guarded it with his life and he guarded it still.

'Paola,' he said. 'I never spoke of it before. I should have.'

'It doesn't matter Wilf,' I said. 'Maybe tonight was the right time. Now, shall I make you a cup of tea? And I think I spotted a packet of chocolate biscuits in the cupboard.'

'That would be lovely, lass.' He smiled for the first time in days and patted my hand.

I was angry as I filled the kettle and found a decent amount of biscuits.

How many more times do we have to say, 'Never again' before we realise the futility of it all? Oh Wilf, no one could ever imagine the horror that you lived through!

Tea was brewed, and I picked up the tray. 'Tea up, Wilf! Look, I found...' Wilf lay still, a look of peace on his face, his eyes half-open in a mask of death. I closed them gently. His hands were lovingly clasped around the little soapstone bowl. Later that night, I'd make sure it went with him to his resting place, where nightmares, hunger and cruelty no longer existed.

Chapter 9

'Pao, I need to talk to you.' It was two months since the night with Wilf and the whole thing hadn't been far from my mind. It's funny how some patients are so easily forgotten, and yet some leave an indelible mark on your soul. I asked myself how a person begins to live a normal life after an experience like that. How do you start to be a man or woman again when all you are is a number tattooed on your forearm? How do you learn to trust…to love again?

Shelagh interrupted these thoughts. 'Pao, are you listening?'

'Yes, of course,' I said, sitting up on the bed where I'd been lazing when she'd come in.

'I've been thinkin.' We're nearly at the end of our training, so we are.'

'Don't remind me!'

'I know, Pao, but before the exams… God help us.' She crossed herself, a gesture of habit not devotion. 'I was thinking of going back home during the three weeks' leave we have before the finals. By the way, what've you chosen for your options?'

Options were decided in the middle of year three. For the last four months of training, we could choose where we wanted to work. It was a taster for what we'd like to do after we qualified. A dip-your-toe-in-the-water before the final dive in. When and *if* we qualified, there'd be no sudden shock of being thrown into something completely unfamiliar. Today, it all happens with indecent haste. It's more *if* you can get a job, not about choosing *where*. In those days, you were expected to stay for at least a year as loyalty to the hospital that had the expense of training you. I was off to do childcare for a month and then out with the community midwife for the rest. My interest in midwifery had grown despite the encounter with the vet.

I'd rushed in with our hospital cat who I believed was dying. To my embarrassment, 'he' turned out to be a 'she' and was about to have kittens. I never lived it down. That incident was responsible for my meeting Robbie, so all the ribbing was worth it. Midwifery would show me how to recognise the basics at least! But, before that we had to take all our holiday allowance in one go: three glorious weeks together, before returning to take our finals. I think Matron expected we'd spend it revising. Fat chance! It would be more about catching up on sleep and drinking ourselves silly.

'What are you going to do after finals, Shelagh?'

'I'm going back to geriatrics.'

'Are you crazy?' I asked, laughing. I was well-aware of how much she loved the old ones, though it wasn't for me. But Shelagh had a gentleness about her that soothed the most agitated old chap, often taking along her guitar to sing to them. To me, it seemed a drudge of a job, but she adored it, from the soiled beds to the mashed-up food and false teeth. The smell alone had been enough to put me off. It was not an experience I'd forget in a hurry.

'Getting back to what I came for, Pao,' she began, perching on the edge of the bed and crossing her long legs. 'I'd love you to come home with me – that's if you've nothing planned.'

'Oh, Shelagh, I couldn't. It'd be an intrusion.'

'It would never! Mammy and Da are desperate to meet you and me brother Declan is well sick of hearing your name. I've told him so much about you, so I have. Will you at least think about it?'

I thought for all of five seconds. 'Shelagh, I'd love to come. If you're sure it wouldn't be too much of an imposition.'

'Of course not,' she said with a huge grin. 'I wouldn't have asked you otherwise and our Declan will be that made up to meet you.'

I couldn't help noticing how often 'our Declan' had been brought up in our conversations of late. I sighed and shook my head. Shelagh's ham-fisted attempts at subterfuge were a little transparent to say the least. If she was trying to fix me up with her brother, it was having the opposite effect. A few weeks ago, I'd started counting how many times 'our Declan' got woven into every conversation – no matter how it had begun. It was 'Declan this' and 'Declan that' and 'Oh, Pao, that is *so* endearing what you just did. I know our Declan would find it so, he would.' There was nothing subtle about Shelagh and I *would* go to Ireland with her.

It was a lovely thought from a good friend who'd stuck with me through thick and thin, and one day I'd find a way to repay her. But that's where friendship stopped. I drew a line at getting romantically involved with Shelagh's brother – not if he was the most gorgeous man in the world and even though she was the best friend anyone could have.

The following Saturday we booked the ferry.

Chapter 10

London might have been enjoying the 'swinging sixties', with its free love, and boast trendy boutiques in the Kings Road and Carnaby Street, but it was half a world away from the sleepy little village where I grew up.

At school, I can only remember one girl whose parents were separated, and it seemed scandalous. Everyone was married – or they seemed to be. I don't suppose they were and I'm sure a good many were living 'over t'brush' while calling themselves Mr and Mrs. A sense of pride was much more important in those days. If your parents weren't married, you were a bastard – end of subject. This was rural Derbyshire with its farmsteads, country lanes and fields of pretty, wild flowers, and free love hadn't reached us.

It may be a well-worn cliché, but where we lived, no one *needed* to lock their doors. Everyone knew what everyone else was doing and a stranger would have stood out immediately. This is where I grew up with a mother, father and three sisters, just another child who went to the village school. It was a kind, safe place, where people were courteous to each other. The bereaved were supported – a bit of washing here, a fresh pie there or a quick call to see if any shopping was needed or a shirt ironing. We shared what we had. The fifties were hard times after the war. Some things were still rationed, but sweets were freely available from 1953. The general store had a wonderful array of penny chews, candy bars, tiger nuts and all the rest. There was a post office, three pubs and a butcher's shop.

I was an odd child – the one who had imaginary friends; the one who saw things that weren't there; heard things no one else could. I must have driven my parents to near-distraction, though they never made me *feel* different. I can remember conversations that ended abruptly when I appeared though. Eyes would follow me down the street until I was out of sight and they could resume. But maybe I imagined that too.

The butcher's wife had first-hand experience of my strangeness. Old Mrs Wild was quite a portly woman who served in the shop whilst husband Jim was 'butcherin' in t'back'. She wore a huge flowery apron and bib that went over her head, crossed and tied behind her back. A typical farmer's wife, she'd an extremely ruddy face from the outdoor life. My mother referred to it as 'country healthy'. She wore her long hair in two plaits that wound around in circles to cover each ear, not unlike headphones. I was fascinated how they stayed put.

'What shall we have for tea today, Paola?' asked my mother as we stood by the counter, the glass polished and gleaming until you could see your reflection. I smiled up at my mother before looking past the old lady.

'What do *you* think we should have for tea today, Olivia?' I asked.

Mrs Wild caught a sharp breath, and pulled her shawl tightly around her shoulders, the tiny grey hairs on her neck standing rigid. 'And what do *you* know of O-Olivia, child?' She paled, her sweet, but diminutive voice stumbling over the name.

'Why, she's your little girl,' I said simply. 'She lives with the angels.'

The old lady's hands trembled as she weighed out a pound of sausages.

I didn't understand why she couldn't see the pretty child who peeped from behind her mother's skirts, her golden curls dancing when she moved. 'Why doesn't she see her?' I asked mother when we were outside the shop.

My mother sighed, one of her deep indulgent ones and crouched to my level. 'I know you see things, my darling. Things that other people can't. But maybe it's better to keep it to yourself, until you're older.'

I *didn't* understand, not for a long time. But I was learning quickly that adults did not approve. The stare the butcher's wife gave me had been less than friendly. My mother, though gentle, was probably right. Perhaps I should keep quiet.

Years later, I discovered that Mrs Wild *had* lost a small child

to meningitis, long before she'd come to the village.
Her name had been Olivia.

Chapter 11

I remembered Belmont children's home from my childhood. All the children living there attended our village school. They were often lonely, disruptive kids who'd been taken from their families and moved to the safety Belmont afforded – for whatever reason. Sometimes it was for protection due to neglect and cruelty or family breakdown and bereavement.

My mother was a dinner lady at the local school and had a special place in her heart for these children. Her mothering instincts always stretched beyond our immediate family. On Sundays, she'd send my dad out to fetch one or two for tea with us, on a rota system. We never knew who we'd be sitting down with from one week to the next, but mum cherished every one of them. So, when I chose childcare as one of my options, Belmont was the obvious placement. All our old clothes ended up there for the children – sometimes as I recall, before we'd finished wearing them.

I arrived on a wet, Monday morning to start my two-month placement, disgruntled that we still had to wear uniform.

The staff consisted of a house-mother and house-father and assorted village women employed as nannies. I don't know what credentials these women had, apart from having children of their own, but they weren't formal. No CRB checks then, beyond a quick ask of the local police whether you were an escaped murderer on the run! Schedule One offenders hadn't been heard of. The best things we can give to children don't always come with a certificate. Love, kindness, attention, and a soft welcoming lap are all that's required and the ability to deal with tears, tantrums, wet beds, snotty noses, and the odd infestation of nits. You had to be able to break up the occasional fight and have the patience and diplomacy of a saint. Overall, a very skilled job! Did anyone know I was only just twenty-years-old with little experience of any of the above when they put me in charge of the O'Flanagans?

Everyone in the locality had heard of the O'Flanagans. They were an Irish tinker family who had ten children, the brood of Mary-Mae and Willy, only twenty-eight years old, the pair of them. No time at all had been lost on the breeding front.

They all lived in a large – very large – caravan just outside Sheffield close to the M1. Willy came home one night rolling drunk and started a row with his wife that finished with him knocking her backwards through the caravan window, breaking both her arms. He'd been arrested, and it had taken four policemen to take him into custody as Willy was a big bloke. Whilst Mary-Mae was hospitalised the ten children were taken into care.

They arrived the day after me and a scruffier bunch would have been hard to imagine. They stood in line in order of height like a one-in-four incline, dirty, and not in the best of temper. The girls wore no knickers and had all peed in their wellington boots. This was to be the first of many challenges I'd face at Belmont if I'd but known. It was like a roll call and went like this in order of age.

Billy (10), Jonny (9), Sammy and Bobby – twins (8), Mary (6), Freddie (5), Jilly (4), Wendy (3), Katie (2) and Lizzie, who was 10 months.

Billy stood in arrogant defiance, clearly the head of the family in the absence of his father. Dirt of unknown origin was smeared liberally across his face.

'You must be Billy,' I began softly, bending to his level.

'Sod off, Miss,' was the reply, heavily accented with the Northern Irish brogue.

'Would you like to introduce your family?' I asked pleasantly.

'Go feck yourself!' I decided to ignore his obvious charm.

Mary held the baby like a protective little mother. 'She'll be wantin' her milk, Miss. She's very hungry and...'

'Yes, Mary, don't you worry now, we'll get her some very soon,' I said moving along the line.

'So is I, Miss. We all is, Miss,' Mary continued. I looked at

Billy for his affirmation. He turned away. 'Oh, don't pay no heed to our Billy, Miss. He's a feckin' Proddy, so he is.'

'I see,' I said, nodding sagely. 'So, that's the problem.' I'd no idea what a Proddy was – feckin' or otherwise, but it didn't sound very nice and I got the distinct impression it wasn't a term of endearment.

Jonny spoke up after stepping forward as if on parade. 'We're all of us Catholics, you see, Miss.'

I glanced up and down the line. 'You don't say.'

'Yes, I do, Miss,' he went on with some indignation. 'That's why there's a lot of us, you see. And me mammy, she's up the Liffie again, so she is. Da says tis all the doing of the little people.'

'I see.' I nodded. 'I expect *everyone* is hungry then...except perhaps you, Billy?' I paused to look at him. 'You won't be interested in any of the delicious chocolate biscuits I happen to have brought with me today?'

He turned his back with a loud, 'Feck off.'

'But, first,' I said, 'we have to do something. You all must have a bath!' Seven panic-stricken faces peered back at me. The youngest three probably didn't understand the implications of soap and water.

'But...but...' stammered Bobby, one of the twins. 'T'aint nobody's *birthday*, Miss. Not Katie or Wendy or Jilly, Miss. We only have a bath when it's somebody's birthday.'

'Well,' I said, 'we'll just have to pretend that it's *everybody's* birthday. So, all the girls come along with me.' They followed me up the stairs slowly, *very* slowly. Patiently, I waited several times while everyone caught up. They stood watching me with worried looks as I ran the bath, then added a good slug of bubble bath, and swirled it around. That did it! With cries of delight, sullen faces were suddenly transformed as they watched the increasing foam with wonder. Clothes were divested at speed and small bodies launched into the huge bath.

The water quickly changed to a grey colour as layer upon layer of muck was soaked off. Dirty urchin faces were transformed into pink angelic ones, hair revealed to be almost white-blonde and impossibly curly, unlike the matted mess that sprouted from their heads before. Just for good measure I gave them all a quick nit comb afterwards. They seemed to enjoy the attention. I suppose coming from such a large family, *that* luxury was rare.

The brood were all dressed in clean nightgowns and returned to the kitchen where they devoured cocoa and chocolate biscuits without a word. Then, Mary, Jilly, Wendy, Katie, and baby Lizzie were settled in little beds side by side in the largest bedroom on the first floor, with space for Lizzie's cot in the middle of them. She'd also been bathed and swaddled in a soft, pink blanket and, after her bottle, was sleeping, thumb in her mouth. I dimmed the lights.

If I entertained any notion this was a triumph, I soon forgot it. The boys were a different matter. All small boys have an inbuilt aversion to soap and water, but this lot? It was like trying to wash a load of tomcats with claws drawn, in a river.

The younger ones were terrified and stood in the bath shivering as if every drop of water was about to make them vanish from the face of the earth. So, it was a quick sponge down and into clean pyjamas with me trying not to notice they still belonged to the Blackfoot tribe! The dirt was so ingrained it'd take more than one bath to soak it off.

The only one still wearing his grimy overcoat was Billy. He stood frowning and defiant by the bathroom door.

'Come on, Billy,' I said, 'clothes off.'

I expected another tirade of obscenities, but he looked scared, his lip quivering. He burst into tears. Great heart-rending sobs sent clean tracks running down his cheeks. 'Billy,' I said, lowering myself to where he sat on the floor. 'Whatever's the matter?' He backed away till he reached the wall. 'Billy, no one's going to make you do anything you don't want. But look mate, Mr and Mrs Andrews won't let you get into one of their clean beds with all this muck on you. So, you'll have nowhere to sleep...and no supper...will you? If you don't like the bath, you can have a good strip wash, just so long as you're clean.'

'But, Miss,' he whispered between sniffs. 'I mustn't take me clothes off.'

'Why not, Billy?'

'You's a *girl*, Miss!'

I laughed. 'I think I'm a bit old for that, Billy. Are you shy?'

He wiped his nose on the sleeve of his coat. 'Aw no, Miss. I'm not frightened of showing meself. It's just that...that...me dad said he'd take his belt to me if ever I did.'

'Why would he say that, Billy?'

He wrestled with the question for a few moments before blurting out. 'Cos...cos...you's from the Social, Miss.'

'No, Billy,' I said gently. 'I'm *definitely not* from the Social.' He looked up from the floor where his gaze had been directed for the past few minutes.

'You sure you's not from the Social?'

'No, Billy, I'm a nurse. I'm here to help people and you can trust me.'

Still unsure, he looked deeply into my eyes and found no lies there. He began to take off his clothes.

'There now,' I said. 'That wasn't too bad, was it?' I coated the flannel with Pears soap and washed his face, rubbing it over his hair, and under all that dirt and frowning was a handsome little boy. I washed his arms and chest and handed him the sponge to do his personal bits, turning my back in deference to his modesty.

'Done, Miss.' He handed me back the discoloured sponge.

'Tell you what, Billy, why don't you call me Paola? That's my name you see, not Miss or Nurse. I'd really like it if you'd call me Paola...now we're friends.' After all, I hadn't heard a 'feck' for at least ten minutes. 'Now turn around, Billy and I'll wash your back.' Saucer-like, fearful eyes gazed into mine again. 'Yes, Billy, what is it?'

'Miss...err...Paola, can you keep secrets?' His voice was a mere whisper.

'I think so, yes.' Slowly he turned, and I gasped, hands going to my mouth. Despite the dirt, it was obvious this little boy had been savagely beaten. 'Oh, Billy,' I said sinking to the floor. Long red wheals criss-crossed his back. There were older ones that had healed into pink scars and new injuries with blood only recently congealed. 'What was it?' I asked quietly. 'A belt? A stick? Who did this to you, Billy?'

He lowered his eyes, ashamed. 'Da said if I ever took me clothes off he'd...' Fear filled those childlike eyes. No wonder he was afraid of the Social, though I doubt he knew what it was. This child must've had the fear of God put into him if he ever told or let anyone see.

'Was it Da, Billy? Did Da do this to you?' I kept my voice

deliberately even. If I'd reacted in the expected way, with horror, I fear he'd have said nothing more and I needed him to talk to me.

He nodded, still facing the wall. Gently, I took him by the shoulders and turned him around to face me. 'Why?'

'I'm naughty, you see. I'm the oldest and should be able to do things.'

'What things, Billy?'

'Be responsible for the little ones when Ma and Da are out, but they fight and sometimes break things and then Da says it's all my fault and I have to be punished for them, because they are too little and...' His voice tailed off.

'And he belts you?'

The boy nodded and hung his head. I was horrified at this child being used as a whipping boy.

Billy suddenly grabbed my arm. 'You'll keep me secret, won't you – or I'll get more. Da said if I ever told a soul, he'd half-kill me, so he did.'

I cleaned his wounds and helped him into his pyjamas. 'Billy,' I said, 'I'm going to make you a solemn promise. But first, I must tell you that this is one secret I can't keep.' I held up my finger at his alarmed expression. 'I want you to listen to me because I promise that your father will never do this to you again – and I never break my promises.'

'You just did, Miss,' he said with tears in his eyes.

I tucked him in with his brothers and sat by the bed until he slept. Then, I went straight to the house-mother and house-father and told them the horrific story.

Next day, they called in the police and the children were made wards of court. There would be detailed physical examinations for other signs of abuse. The parents would be arrested and charged, the father most likely jailed. The children would go into permanent foster care, not necessarily together. All those implications were not lost on me and it didn't sit easily. I'd single-handedly been responsible for the family being split up. I tossed and turned that night, wrestling with my conscience. At 2am I was in the kitchen making tea for the second time that night. The boiler groaned and gurgled as I sat at the table with the day's events going around in my head like a carousel.

Why is everything so difficult? Resting table my head on the scrubbed pine, I closed my eyes. This is where I fell in love with Robbie. I didn't know it then, but it *was* here in this building, this room with its creaks and moans. It seemed a whole world away. As if to compound the sad memory, the cat awoke and sprung from the boiler onto my lap, purring softly. I shivered, not from cold, but there *were* ghosts here. They were the ghosts of lost love and the happiness we'd had. The cat nuzzled at my hand to be stroked and I caressed her soft fur. It was at times like this I missed him more than ever, though not quite so raw now. The emotion had softened to sadness and a loneliness often hard to bear. Like the empty-arms syndrome of a mother who's lost her child. My arms were empty too, but I wasn't ready to let go yet. I had to hold on to his memory and, if that meant Robbie was unable to move on, well...I wasn't at all sure I wanted him to.

'Selfish,' I said aloud. 'Selfish!' I didn't care. I needed him. How I needed him. I wanted the warm sensation of his arms around me like the night Linnie brought him back to me here in the kitchen. I carried the echo of his voice in my head.

'We are given what we need, Pao, not necessarily what we want. The two are not the same.'

I sipped my tea and returned to my conscience and the family I was about to tear apart. No single foster home would be able to take all ten children. They'd be split up and would never see each other again. What had I done? Fresh tears fell.

There was a waft of Blue Grass perfume under my nose. I sat up and looked around with a feeling of warmth and expectation, my eyes wide. 'Linnie?' I whispered. 'Linnie, is that you?' The smell became stronger and a warm glow settled around me in the dim early morning light of the huge kitchen. A tiny ball of light began to dance, bouncing from one wall to the other and back again becoming a golden orb that settled in front of me. Could it really be her, my friend from long ago? 'Linnie?' I asked again.

'Yes, I'm here.' The voice was a mere soft whisper behind my ear.

I closed my eyes and breathed slowly and steadily knowing she was there. 'I'm in trouble, Linnie,' I said.

'No, you're not.' Her voice was as soft as swan's-down.

'I've split up a family.'

'Did *you* beat that child, Paola?'

'No, of course not.'

'You've protected them.'

'But they'll be separated and sent away.'

'You don't know that, and is it worse than being beaten half to death by a drunken father? The mother can't protect them, so you must.'

'I wish it hadn't been me!'

'Did anyone *tell* you this job would be easy?'

'No. No one said that.'

'There'll be many more times when you'll have to stand up and be counted, Paola.'

'Oh God, let's hope not.'

'And much worse times when you're the only person who stands in the way, the only hope a child has.'

'How do I cope with that, Linnie?'

'You know...' The lights began to dance again. 'There was a time when children weren't believed and accused of lying. No one owns their children, Pao. They're not chattels to be done with as we see fit. We're only allowed to borrow them for a little while.' It was an echo of Linnie's short time on earth. My tears flowed again. 'What do you think would have happened if you hadn't told, Pao?'

'I imagine the boy would have continued to be beaten until...'

'Until what?'

'Until he was old enough to fight back...or one of the smaller ones took his place. Or until he was killed by his father, when, one day he went too far.'

'Then be proud of what you've prevented.'

'I'll be criticised,' I said, with a deep sigh.

'Not by anyone who matters. Do you really care if someone calls you a busybody or an interfering bitch?'

I paused, biting my bottom lip. 'I care what people *think* of me, doesn't everyone?'

'The only thing that's important is those children were at risk and now they're safe – and that's down to you for having the courage to stand up and be counted.'

'I'm so tired!' I said rubbing my eyes. I could imagine her sitting there opposite me, arms folded the way she used to, auburn hair falling to her waist. I thought of the freckles she hated so much, always trying to blot them out with Panstick make-up. I could imagine her looking at me and smiling. 'Linnie, are you smiling?'

'Of course I'm smiling. I always smiled when you were around, Pao. You made me laugh.'

'Why?'

'Dunno. I suppose you're a naturally funny person.'

I took a deep breath. 'If I open my eyes will I be able to see you?'

'Why don't you try?'

'Oh, I...'

'Not scared of little old me, are you?'

'It's not that.'

'Then open your eyes.'

Slowly, I obeyed. It was like the first time I'd seen her the Christmas after she died. She was just the same. What *did* I expect? That she'd changed her clothes and had her hair done? She read my thoughts.

'Don't need any of those things now, Pao. Nothing changes.'

'Will you grow old like me?'

'Not in the way you mean.'

I laughed. 'What no wrinkles and a few extra chins?'

'It doesn't work like that.'

My eyes widened unable to tear my gaze away from her. 'How does it work, Linnie?'

Those blue, mesmerising eyes stared back. 'You see what you remember best.'

'I've so many questions to...'

'They'll all be answered – in time.'

Chapter 12

I awoke with a start, my forehead still resting on the pine kitchen table. Massaging my stiff neck, I rushed upstairs to get ready for work, legs protesting. I bathed and had to miss breakfast. If there was one thing I hated it was being late.

The O'Flanagans were nearly unrecognisable from the family who'd come to Belmont two days before. They were all sitting around having breakfast, clean and with elbows off the table. Each head bore the tell-tale signs of nit treatment, slicked back in the case of the boys, and the girls pinned up on top. It would be washed out later and there would be no more itching and scratching. Who knows how long they'd had to endure the infestation, and all for the sake of a couple of bottles of lotion and a good comb.

They looked content, not anxious and awkward like the day before. I marvelled at how well they'd adapted. But children do when safe, fed and loved, and the Andrews would see to it they *were* loved the same as all the others in their care. That was okay for the present. I worried about what would happen when the time came for someone to break the news they wouldn't be returning to their parents.

'May I see you, Miss Green?' Mr Andrews popped his head round the dining room door. 'Come into the sitting room later when you've some time to spare.'

Oh...I'm in trouble. I thought. Isn't it strange our first reaction as nurses when called to the office is *What have I done?* We must have terribly guilty consciences, never assuming it's for praise. Experience has taught us it rarely is. We're very good at telling each other off, laying down the law and chastising. It would be great if we were *equally* good at offering praise with a quick, 'Well done. That was a great job you did there.'

I wasn't sure whether to stand or sit in front of Mr Andrews and shuffled from foot to foot in anticipation of what was to come.

'Oh, for heaven's sake, Paola, *do* sit.' He indicated a nearby comfortable chair. 'This isn't a visit to Matron or the hospital hanging committee!' I sat up straight, hands in my lap feeling the need to show a bit of formality. 'Good grief girl, relax will you?'

'Sorry, sorry…' I stammered taking the initiative. 'It's about the O'Flannagans, isn't it?' A smile played at the corners of his mouth, though it didn't reach his eyes as he watched me carefully. He was about fifty and balding, a tall man and pleasant to look at, his grey eyes kind. A wise old owl was what came to mind; a man who spent all his working life caring for other people's children with unending patience and understanding.

He sat in the armchair and leaned forward, elbows resting on his knees. 'I want you to listen carefully to me, Paola. We've been watching you these last few days, me and Mrs Andrews. You've been torturing yourself.' His eyes searched my face. 'Am I right?'

'Well, a bit,' I said, nodding. 'I suppose I have.'

'I think it's a more than a bit, so I want you to do something.' He beckoned me with his finger. 'Come with me.' He got up and walked to the door and held it open for me. I followed him to the office. That's what it said on the door, but it was more like a sitting room. The only reference to actual office work was the desk in front of a large picture window looking out over the playroom. On this Saturday afternoon, it was busy with children doing various activities and the inevitable arguments from time to time. Several 'aunties' were presiding over this family atmosphere. It was not contrived, but like any other home across the country. I wondered how they managed it with children coming and going all the time. Some stayed only a few days while other arrangements were made, others for a longer period.

'Let's watch for a while,' he said. We sat by the window. Toys were plentiful, and I doubted some of the children had seen so many. 'Look,' he said after a few minutes. 'Happy, healthy children, yes?'

'Yes,' I said. 'They seem perfectly happy.'

He pointed to a couple of children playing on a see-saw. 'That little girl and boy, do you see them, Paola? They are called Jenny and Philip and they are twins. Watch them for a moment and tell me what you see.' He paused to smile at me. 'Now I'm *really* testing your powers of observation.' He raised an eyebrow, his grey eyes returning to the children in question.

I watched the two five-year-olds squealing with delight as each end of the see-saw reached its zenith, then bumped down again to yet more whoops of fun. 'They seem happy enough,' I said.

'What about trusting?' he asked.

'Yes, they seem so.'

'Well-adjusted, Paola?'

I thought for a moment before replying. 'Yes, very.'

He sat, turning his chair to face me. 'What do you base that on?'

I paused to consider. 'Their demeanour and the way they play together. They seem to get on well, but that's twins. It's either loving or loathing. At this age, I suppose, it's just someone to play with who's always been there.'

'Do you see anything wrong, just by using your eyes and looking?'

I watched them playing for a few more minutes. Everything seemed well. 'If I had to be pernickety, Mr Andrews, I'd say they only have eyes for each other and don't interact much with the other children. It's as though no one else is in the room.'

'Why so formal, Paola? Please call me Derek.'

'Derek,' I repeated and smiled.

'That's much better. We're all here for the same purpose and that's to give these children better than they've had so far. How do *you* see this place? Come on, blurt out the first thoughts that come into your head.'

I laughed. 'I see. A psychological exercise for the most recent *and* temporary member of staff.'

'Not really, though a good instinct is important, especially with children. It's even more so with the kind of children that come into our care. You need to look beyond what's obvious.'

'On that, my knowledge is limited,' I said with an apologetic look.

'I can't agree with you, Paola. Like I said, I've been watching you closely and I think you have an aptitude for understanding children. That's rare in someone of your age.'

'Can't imagine where it came from!' I said, nonplussed. 'My younger sister and I used to fight like tomcats when we were both at home.'

'And you don't need to have children yourself to understand, because you were a child once. As we grow up and develop our adult values it's all too easy to forget how we thought as children, and what was important to us at the time.'

'It wasn't too long ago or at least it doesn't seem so.'

'Correct.' He paused. 'Now let me see, Paola Green... How old are you? Twenty-ish?' I nodded and smiled. 'Play along with me and let me test *my* powers of observation.'

'Go on,' I said, amused, relaxing now, sitting back and folding my arms.

'You come from a stable, happy family background with three siblings and you are – let me think – the *third* child?

I thought it was a good guess and smiled indulgently, raising an eyebrow. 'Your parents probably had the first two followed by a break before more came along, making you the first child of the second wave.' I wrinkled my brow in surprise at another accurate guess. This man was starting to impress me. 'How am I doing, Paola Green?'

'How *can* you know that?' I gave a snort of laughter.

'You're too young to have been born during the war, but you're frugal and dislike waste. I noticed at meal times. That's the influence of older sisters whose parents have known lean times. *Your* parents are more lenient with the two of you and your older sisters resent it.'

I stared at him, my mouth dropping open.

He went on. 'Your stockings are new and not mended. Your shoes are sensible but polished carefully and you've standards other than those imposed by Matron. But you like to push the boundaries now and then. Oh yes, your eyes are carefully lined with kohl so as not to be too obvious that you're wearing make-up – and lipstick. Oh, Nurse Green, slap your wrist! Matron would most *definitely* not approve. Close your mouth, Paola. It's okay, I won't dob you in!'

I gasped in shock and he laughed heartily. 'How on earth do you know all that?' I said, finding my voice at last.

He leaned back in the chair, hands linked at the back of his head. 'You have the confidence of a third child. I expect you pay board at home and your parents allow you a little money for yourself for luxuries like lipstick, though I bet your mum still doesn't like you wearing it for work.'

'I give in,' I said. '*How* do you know that?'

'From your manner *and* your manners, the way you carry and present yourself. One can read so much from a person's appearance. When these children come to us, we have a little to go on, though not the whole story by any means. So, we look, listen, and deduce – a bit like Sherlock Holmes and Dr Watson. But, there's something much more important.'

'What's that?' We were back to the serious side of things now.

'It's the art of cajoling. Getting people to let things slip they don't even realise they've told us. You mentioned your sisters at dinner last night. I bet you don't remember.'

'No, I don't! And the lipstick?'

'I saw you apply another coat as you dashed up the drive this morning!'

'Ahhh…and what about all that Freudian stuff?'

He laughed and wiped his eyes. 'Joseph Green, your dad. I often have a few pints with him on a Friday night in the Bull's Head.' He raised his hands in a submissive gesture. 'Elementary, my dear Paola!'

'Oh, you beast,' I cried and we both burst out laughing, sharing the joke that was clearly on me.

'Now back to the business in hand,' said Derek. 'Those two children. Can you remember the last thing you said before I began taking the Michael out of you?'

'I said they'd only eyes for each other.'

'When Jenny and Philip were removed from their home, the police found padlocks high up on the doors. What do you suppose they were for, Paola?' I shook my head. 'Their mother used to bring her men back and the children were made to watch.'

My hands went up to the sides of my face in horror and disbelief. 'But…why?'

'Abuse. Sexual abuse is all about control. Don't ever believe that it's always the men who are the perpetrators because some women are quite capable of the most horrendous acts. The mother's actions were saying, 'Look what I have to do to provide for you. You *will* watch you little bastards. This is your fault."

'But they didn't ask to be born,' I protested, trying without success to remove images of what they must have seen from my mind. To a child, the sex act must look like extreme violence and God knows what else they'd seen. They must have thought their mother was being killed over and over. All they had was each other to cling to, and they were still doing that.

Derek looked at me. 'You look as though you could do with a coffee.'

I nodded, finding no words to describe what I felt. 'How did they come to be here, Derek?' I asked, unable to drag my eyes from the pair happily playing together on the see-saw.

'A rather heroic teacher at the infant's school,' he said sipping coffee. She noticed their behaviour with each other was sexualised. Such behaviour in children so young can only be learned from having witnessed it. Five-year-olds don't exhibit adult gestures of that nature. I won't go into further detail, Paola. She went straight to the headmistress who told her she was overreacting because she was new to the job. I *said* she was heroic and I meant it, because she didn't let it go and refused to be silenced. She knew something wasn't quite right and trusted her instincts, thank God. When the police broke in with Social Services in tow, they couldn't believe their eyes. The mother confessed, unable to deny it – caught red-handed so to speak.'

'And what happens now?' I asked.

'They've been with us for fifteen weeks and it's going to be a long haul, but slowly they're learning to be children again. It's all going to take time.'

'But they'll never be sent back to her?'

'I doubt that very much.' He shook his head. 'They'll be fostered and then adopted, hopefully together.'

'But they'll be kept together?'

'Nothing's a certainty, I'm afraid.'

I was still a little stunned at what lurked beneath the surface of this seemingly lovely place.

'Now Paola, look here, more observation for you.' Derek finished his drink and placed the empty mug on the desk. 'I want you to think back to yesterday's tea and the little boy who wasn't eating – the one we were trying hard to ignore. Sorry, I'm a real slave driver once I get going.'

'Michael Phipps,' I said. 'He kept getting off his chair and crawling under the table?'

'The very same,' said Derek. 'What a naughty boy, don't you think, Paola?'

'Well...'

'Come now, what's *your* opinion?'

'That he wasn't hungry, perhaps?'

'Oh, he was hungry all right.'

'Then why wasn't he eating, Derek?'

'He thinks he's not allowed to.'

'Not allowed...? Why?' My face was reddening.

'Don't worry,' he held up a placating hand. 'We feed him after everyone else has left.' Derek sat back and linked his fingers at the back of his head.

'I don't understand. Why should he believe that?'

'When the police went into the house and found this boy, he was cowering in a corner of the kitchen, filthy, apart from his face and hands. They were spotlessly clean.

'Sorry, Derek, I still don't understand.'

'No? He can't use a knife, fork or spoon and he sits under the table.' Derek counted off the points by raising his fingers in turn. 'Any clues yet, Paola?'

I shook my head, puzzled.

Derek went on. 'It would be very easy to dismiss him as just a naughty little boy with no manners, but you have to look beyond the obvious. Things are rarely what they seem.' He paused for a moment. 'Okay, I'll explain. His mother had been a loving, single mum until one day she met a man who she became completely obsessed with. He seemed great at first, attentive, charismatic and good looking. Until the day he moved in. From that moment, the little boy's life became something out of a horror movie. You see, the boy had only ever known there to be him and his mother, and he rebelled against the intrusion of someone who was now demanding his mother's time. He became sullen and naughty – quite naturally. What would you do, Paola if suddenly you'd been replaced in someone's affections?'

'I expect I'd protest, but a child of that age hasn't the words. So, he was punished?'

'Not physically, but then there are many forms of punishment and, once again, this was about control. I am your new man. I live here now, and I will show you by controlling your boy. I will take the responsibility, so leave him to me. You've had the responsibility single-handed. Now I'll do it. It's because I love you. What do you think, Paola? *Is* this a show of love?'

'I'd *never* hand over responsibility of my child to anyone,' I said, shaking my head firmly.

'What...never?' Derek leaned forward, scrutinising my face.

'No,' I said louder and firmer.

'What if then, because of your intransigence you were to risk losing the only man who'd loved you in years? What if you *had* to choose between him and your son?'

'It's no contest. Blood's thicker than water and a mother's love is the most powerful of all. You'd protect your child at all costs.'

'Okay. But what if someone was capable of brainwashing you into believing they knew best, that it was for your own good, because they loved you like no one else loved you?' Derek went on, ignoring my sharp intake of breath. 'Subtle control. It's amazing how often control is linked to child abuse in some way or other. So, he was made to sit under the table to be fed and was made to sleep with the dogs – just until he learned to behave. But it was never good enough because in the eyes of his abuser, there would always be need for further punishment because that's what control is.' Derek paused, his eyes on mine. 'Dirty but with clean hands and face?' He paused for a moment. 'What do animals do after they've eaten?'

'They lick themselves cl.... Oh no, Derek.' Sudden realisation came like a lightning bolt.

'And in time, the dogs accepted him as part of the pack and washed his face and hands clean as they did their own and–'

'Where the hell was the mother in all this?' I exploded. 'Why did she allow that to happen, for God's sake?' I was on my feet, fists clenched, my face burning.

'Good question. Paola...calm please. I'm angry too. Sit down there opposite me and we'll play a little game. Come on, this anger will pass. You can't be objective when you're this wound

94

up. Breathe. That's better.' He handed me a glass of water. 'Now drink that and sit down.'

I did as I was told and presently the anger subsided.

'I'm not going to sit here and pretend this job is easy because that would be doing you a very great disservice. So, let's play a little game. Like charades, only you must close your eyes. I'm going to tell you a story and I want you to pretend you're that person.'

I nodded and did as he asked.

'Now, Paola, you are completely alone in the world save for your son who is four. You've had no adult company since he was born. You've no one to talk to on an adult level and you're broke and desperate. Then, one day, you meet someone. He's nice to you, interested in what you've got to say and, above all, he's good to your boy. He spoils him, buys him the toys and clothes you can't afford. He takes you out, lavishes money on you too. Meals, flowers, spends time with you and, above all, he tells you he loves you. You begin to trust him and before long you find yourself falling in love with him. You can't believe your luck! You relax now because you no longer have the worry about where the next meal is coming from or how you are going to pay the gas bill. He's sees to all that, so you no longer need to think about it. He's yours and you're his and he supplies your every need – you and your boy. You trust him and there's no need for anyone else. Then come the rules. He wants you to go out only when he does. He says he worries about you and needs to know where you are. Why? Because he loves you. He says no one has ever loved you like he does. Can you see where this is going, Paola. I'm that man and I'm taking away your will, your individuality, your freedom. It's because you're mine, all mine, and you do what I tell you to. We buy what I want, we eat when I say, and we go everywhere together – because I love you. You love me, don't you, Paola? Enough to trust me completely? You see, Paola, you're no good on your own. Look what a mess you made of things before I came. That's why I take care of you now, you and the boy. I control every aspect of your life. I control where you go, when you sleep, how you dress, when we make love, because...' Derek suddenly raised his voice, 'because you are worthless without me!'

'Derek, stop please.' I was sweating with panic. 'No more.'

'Okay, Paola,' he continued, softer now, 'you're a strong girl who would never get herself into that situation, or else be able to get out at the first sign of danger, but there are people who can't.'

'Why didn't she just leave and take the boy?'

'Because, slowly she'd been brainwashed into believing she was worthless and *nothing* without the man. She needed him for everything. How could she get away? He'd taken over her home. She was a prisoner in effect, no freedom, no rights, no money, no self-belief. A non-person.'

'So how...?'

'A very brave health visitor who, when turned away just kept coming back until one day, the man had fallen asleep upstairs.

It took a mere few minutes for her to realise what was happening, and she took a hell of a beating when he woke unexpectedly and found her there. He split her lip and when she refused to leave, broke her jaw with a single punch. The shock of this attack on another woman had a profound effect. The mother grabbed her son and ran screaming into the street.'

'Where is she now?'

'That's not our problem.'

I stared.

'But she's safe. The child comes first and last. If you only take away one thing from today, remember this. The child *always* comes first. I've heard it said, time after time, that a child is always better off with its parents. Don't ever believe that, because my response is to ask them to remember Maria Cauldwell; beaten, starved, and murdered. Was *she* better off with her parents?' It didn't need a reply. 'It's a fine line we tread, Paola, and every day we walk a precarious path, always condemned by someone, whatever we do. So, to answer your question of about an hour ago,' he said with a glance at his watch, 'if you can remember what that question was, you asked if this was about the O'Flannagans. Well, yes – absolutely! *You* have a great deal in common with that school teacher and health visitor.'

'Have I?'

'Oh yes. For without their courage and yours, there would have *been* no end to the suffering of these children, until perhaps they were murdered.'

I flinched at the thought.

Derek went on. 'And for you to have the strength and tenacity to speak up at your young age is exceptional. You had the courage of your convictions and I'm proud of you, young lady. Never reproach yourself for putting children first. One thing I can promise you though, is that the next time you stick your neck out and all the times after that, it will never get any easier!'

'Someone else told me that. A girlfriend.'

'She was very wise, so listen to her,' said Derek.

'She was...is...and I will.' I smiled for the first time in an hour.

'Oh God, Shelagh, do you realise it's only just over two months to our finals?' The stark reality had just sunk in. 'When we get back from Ireland, we take our finals.'

'Well, Pao, you've put the work in, so what yer worrying about?' Shelagh gave a deep sigh and crossed her long legs.

'I know,' I said, 'but do you think we should take our books to Ireland with us, just to be sure?'

'Will we hell?' huffed Shelagh. 'What we don't know now...well, it's just flippin' hard luck, so it is. Holidays are for sleepin', drinkin', and singin' and not with yer nose in some stuffy old textbook. So, if I were to see you try to take one, so help me, I'll be chuckin' it into the Irish Sea, – and you may be followin' it.'

'Point taken,' I said. 'No books.'

'No,' she wagged her finger. 'Nothin' except a desire to enjoy yerself and nothin' bloody else.'

I laughed at her seriousness. 'You do me good, Shelagh. I don't know how I'd have survived this past year without you.'

'Oh, and none of *that* neither. Our Declan doesn't want to be seein' no grievin' widow, so he doesn't.'

There it was again, 'Our Declan'. I couldn't help but smile.

'Have you packed yet, Pao?'

'Don't be silly,' I said, 'I'm still wearing them. I don't possess *that* many clothes.'

Chapter 13

Trevor Evershall: by naming him such, his parents had clearly not given too much thought to the consequences. He was mercilessly teased at school and ringing in his ears was either 'Trevor forever', on the rare occasions he managed to put a ball in the back of the net, or that ghastly song, 'Green grow the rushes O,' which the other kids adapted to 'One is one, he's on his own and ever Trev shall be so'.

But when he entered the clergy and took holy orders it was, for some, too good an opportunity to miss. The Reverend Trevor Evershall became known as 'Trev the Rev' from the moment he stepped through the hospital gates to take up his post of Church of England chaplain.

He also rode a moped and so became 'Revving Trev, the Rev'. The connotations and jokes the poor man had to suffer were endless. Some bright spark suggested that if he were to get married, it really must be to someone called Beverley. Then, it could be 'Bev and Trev – spouse and Rev'. He bore it all with fortitude and a smile as though it were the first time he'd heard it. But I think he spent his whole life avoiding anyone under thirty called Beverley – just in case.

There were two hospital chaplains and they couldn't have been more different. Representing the Catholic faith was Father Gerrity Flynn. He was known behind his back as 'Grrr' and not without good reason. He was the epitome of a priest: small, round and with a large belly which the belt of his black robe had difficulty in circumnavigating, always appearing to be under great strain – as did Father Flynn. He was a very bad tempered little man who rarely blessed you with a smile, his mouth set in a fixed line of 'eve of destruction' impending doom. Bald, apart from a circle of thin grey hair, he wouldn't have been out of place in a monk's habit and was so short-sighted that his spectacles looked like the bottoms of jam jars. He certainly disapproved of Trevor in his leather bikers' trousers and hooded Parka trimmed with the pelt of some long-dead animal. And definitely not his moped, nor his youth. There was also the *small* matter of Trevor's faith.

Father Flynn believed there *was* only one religion and that was governed by Rome. And in keeping with every war fought over the subject, hostilities between the two were inevitable. We were all merely holding our breath and awaiting the opening salvo.

Shelagh had not so much lost her faith as sent it packing long ago. Ireland was in the throes of the 'Troubles'. The IRA was killing people just because they were of a different faith, and her home in Sligo was very near the border with the north. The threat of being caught up between the warring factions was real. A distant cousin was a guest of Her Majesty in Armagh Prison and Shelagh certainly wanted no part of it – when sober. Nationalism only reared its head when she'd had a few and started to sing. Poor Shelagh had fallen foul of Father Flynn when she'd only been on English soil a fortnight.

He made it his mission to seek out all the Irish student nurses who lived in the nurses' home and, if necessary, drag them kicking and screaming to Sunday Mass to save their souls whilst away from home. Shelagh had told him clearly why he should give her up as a lost cause. Defiantly, she'd tossed her head, hitched up her miniskirt and crossed her shapely legs provoca- tively, at which point his glasses all but steamed up. Then, she leaned forward and placed her cleavage close to his nose and asked him to light her cigarette. The words 'sinful harlot' and 'fallen woman' had been clearly heard, but from that moment he'd avoided her like the plague. He'd obviously marked her as 'one of those terrible Protestant sympathisers to whom he constantly referred.

Shelagh was, in fact, apolitical, having seen what religion could do and how bigoted views and unspeakable acts were carried out in its name. She referred to the nuns at her convent school as the Gestapo for the way they'd administered punish- ment with obvious pleasure, from a ruler rapped across the knuckles to incarceration in the dreaded punishment room. One night, after a very drunken party, she'd recounted it. Jenny Else and I had been sitting on Shelagh's bed, our backs against the wall, finishing off a couple of bottles of barley wine.

'Bitches in penguin suits,' she retorted, 'and they loved every minute of it. Thugs protected by a crucifix!' We were unprepared for what was coming as she continued with a glare at the wall. 'We weren't even allowed to wear shiny, patent shoes. Did you know that?'

'Why the hell not?' asked Jenny, puffing on her cigarette.

'Because,' said Shelagh, lighting one herself and drawing deeply on it, 'the shine may reflect our knickers and *that* my friends might lead to impure thoughts.'

'Oh, my God,' I said, shaking my head.

'Tell me,' said Shelagh, 'just what impure thoughts is a seven-year-old likely to have? They were raving mad, the lot of them. If you made mistakes in class, they were into humiliation. You were called out to the front of the class to put yer hands on the desk. Then they'd beat the backs of them with a large ruler. And if yer were to pull them away at the last moment, the punishment was doubled and sometimes tripled. All in front of your friends too. Me hands were so bruised I could hardly hold a feckin' pencil. Some poor little sods that weren't very bright got beaten till they bled. They sent them outside to stand in the rain and told to pray for their unworthy souls.' We stared. 'Well, *this* unworthy soul had enough one day, and as one of the sisters brought the ruler down, I kicked her hard on the shins with me non-patent shoes, let me tell yer. She fell to the ground screaming hellfire and blazes and three other nuns rushed in and grabbed me. I yelled like a banshee as they dragged me out of the room by the hair and down the stairs to the basement. Two of them stripped off me clothes till I was only wearing me knickers and one unlocked the door with this huge bunch of keys and shoved me inside a tiny room. I was screaming for me ma and they were screaming that I was the daughter of the Devil himself and had to be punished. One of them still had a handful of me hair in her hand, so she did.

'Oh, Shelagh...my God!' was all I could say, both hands over my mouth.

'Yeah. And I'm tellin' yer now that God had nothin' to do

with any of it.'

'Oh, Shelagh,' I repeated, 'how old were you?'

'Nine years old and the swine locked me in a dark room with hardly space to turn around. I expect it had been a cupboard of some sort. It was pitch black save for a small candle fixed to the wall, lighting a big picture of Christ crucified with blood running down his face and side. I screamed and screamed until I'd no voice left. That picture of the Lord seemed to be looking right at me. There was a sign that said, 'Sinners repent before God'. I closed me eyes tight and wet meself.'

Jenny and I looked at her, the horror obvious in our eyes, rendered speechless at how anyone in the name of God could inflict such torture on a small child.

'When they let me out,' said Shelagh, her eyes full of tears now, 'they washed me and put me clothes and shoes back on and I was allowed to go home with the others. When I told Ma, she was horrified and I never went back there again.' She sighed deeply. 'So, you'll forgive me if I think religion stinks.' She stubbed out her cigarette forcefully grinding it into the ashtray until it fell apart. We both jumped off the bed to envelop her in our arms for a group hug. Shelagh never spoke of it again.

The reverend Trevor was only five years out of theological college, where he'd trained in his native Derbyshire. Bleak and exposed to the prevailing winds that whipped across the heather moors, the college stood alone on a hill near Buxton; a cliff edge of mountain limestone that formed part of the backbone of England.

The facility had gained some notoriety with the emergency services as, close by, several new-born babies had been found abandoned over the years. This had been attributed to the lady students at the college, who, when finding themselves pregnant were unable to face the shame. Fertility issues amongst the soon-to-be clergy didn't seem to be a problem – though the outcome was!

After he qualified, Trevor found he'd had enough of the bleak lifestyle the college afforded and took up a post as curate in the East End of London. There was so much poverty and damp housing at that time; he was looking forward to being able to make a difference. But all the idealism of his youthful ambition was impossible to maintain in the dark slums with poor families eking out their hand to mouth existence, and never a shortage of violence on the streets. Try as he might, he found himself impotent to change anything. He'd stayed for two years and his sensitive soul had hated every moment of it, realising he was not suited to life in 'the Smoke'. He longed for the green fields of Derbyshire, sheep moors and the pure clean air, and most of all, for his childhood sweetheart, Becky Rowley – a sheep farmer's daughter from nearby Litton.

Sometimes, at night, when all the children were asleep on the ward, he'd talk to me about his time in the East End and his utter frustration and inability to make a difference. When our extremely elderly hospital chaplain retired, Trevor applied for the post and got it. I'd tell him of Belmont and how idealistic views get knocked out of you. We'd chat like two elderly ladies over a cup of tea. Old heads on young shoulders, our last few years having taught us both so much. Trying to pull hope from disappointment and optimistic humour from tragedy. And we'd laugh because that's a failsafe for all things, always finding the ridiculous, as a way of coping with difficult situations. It provided sanity in a crazy world.

Trevor was home, back on familiar territory and near to his love. His life would have been complete, apart from his nemesis, the unbelievably bad-tempered Father Gerrity Flynn, who he found impossible to avoid. Joint services were held in the hospital chapel every Sunday and they were well attended. I'm convinced people came for the entertainment value, as both had *very* different styles. Father Flynn preached hellfire, damnation, and promised retribution for sin and fornication, while insisting on conducting his part of the service in Latin.

Trevor had a much gentler approach, concentrating on forgiveness and the blessing of our young people. It was a recipe for disaster. Father Flynn would sit hands clasped in his lap occasionally raising his eyes to heaven, crossing himself and tut-tutting throughout. After a few weeks, Trevor could stand it no longer, fearful the congregation were only waiting for a fight to break out and the chance see him maimed with a communion candlestick.

'Paola, I fear we must have separate services,' he confided in me, 'and *that* defeats the object of integration, surely.'

'But Trevor,' I said, 'the two of you don't exactly sing from the same hymn sheet do you, if you'll pardon the pun?'

'Hmmm.' Trevor continued to wrestle with the problem. There seemed to be no solution. Both did their rounds of the wards each morning, doing their best to avoid each other. Father Flynn wouldn't have anything to do with anyone who wasn't Roman Catholic – even if they were taking their last breath and needed a hand to hold. I got the impression that if he did he believed a bolt of lightning would strike him dead. I made a note to nominate him for 'bigot of the year award'.

Trevor was a wanderer, not minding if the patients pulled the covers over their heads and feigned sleep when they saw him coming. He had a cheery word for all and even removed his dog collar to play with the children – always allowing them to win, of course. He helped to feed the smaller ones and spent hours merely stroking the hair of a sick infant. It was during one of my stints on Maggie's – Princess Margaret Ward – that holy war was destined to break out.

It had been a hectic shift. Seven children had been to the operating theatre for various surgery; tonsils and adenoids, circumcisions, and grommets in their ears. All needed lots of attention. Parents didn't stay with children as they do today. The left side of the ward was the medical area with steam tents housing kids with bronchitis and asthma and it was full. Being February, it was damp and cold and most houses lacked central heating. Often these children came from an estate in a poor area of town with its small, overcrowded terraces and the privy across the yard. They had damp bedrooms, draughty, poorly main-tained windows with only a smoky coal fire downstairs. Women with large families were unable go out to work being far too busy caring for a husband and children, so money was always a bit tight.

'Can I do anything to help, Nurse Green?' our newest chaplain asked, his voice gentle.

'Oh, Trevor,' I sighed, my shoulders sinking with relief, 'you are a gift from...' I laughed. 'Well never mind that. You're a gift.'

'Gosh,' he blushed and looked down the ward. 'Why so many little ones?'

'The cold snap, I expect. I don't suppose it's as bad as the East End, but you know how it is. Get them well with steam, physio and antibiotics and send them home to damp, overcrowded houses and a couple of weeks later, back they come again.'

'Shall I start feeding the little ones? Suffer little children, and all that.'

'Yes please, Rev. I think there's too much suffering of little children around here at present.'

Quickly, I handed him a couple of dishes of rice pudding, before he changed his mind. Deftly, he fed the toddlers in their steam tents, each spoonful becoming a big aeroplane going into a hangar or a cuckoo going back into its clock and all with appropriate sound effects. He kept disappearing to the kitchen for further supplies until all were fed.

I stood watching in admiration. 'You know, Trevor, you really have a knack with these little ones.' He smiled, as another rice pudding laden aeroplane made its final approach above the cot, coming safely to land in an awaiting mouth.

'It must be something to do with the dog collar,' he said, touching it gently.

'Mister Twevver,' asked a little voice, 'why are you wearing your dog's collar?'

'He doesn't need it today, pretty baby,' said Trevor gently, 'so I borrowed it. He won't mind.'

'I fink that's silly,' said the child.

'I fink you could be right,' said Trevor, wiping her lips on a tissue.

'That deserves a cuppa,' I said, turning towards the kitchen. I froze.

Coming down the corridor in his long cassock was Father Flynn. 'Penguin alert! Quick Trevor,' I said over my shoulder. 'It's your nemesis.'

'Oh bugger,' he whispered under his breath, looking for a hiding place.

'Good afternoon, Father Flynn.' I forced a very false smile. 'May I give you some coffee?' That would keep him in the office for a bit whilst Trevor made his escape, though I did wonder whether it was wise to provide him with a weapon – and a hot one at that.

'Thank you, Nurse. That would be most agreeable.' He sat at the desk, hands clasped across his capacious belly. 'Now, where is my list?'

'Sorry?'

'My list? The daily list of Catholic children on this ward?'

Daylight dawned, and I scrabbled around in the loose papers on Sister's desk. 'Oh, here it is. No, that seems to be Sister's shopping list. Sorry.' He raised his eyes to heaven. 'The junior nurse should have done it, but clearly she hasn't had time, so while you enjoy your coffee, I'll do it for you. We've been exceptionally busy. Sorry, err…sugar and milk?'

'Four sugars.'

I smiled. No wonder his belt was straining.

With his over-sweetened coffee cradled in his lap, I grabbed the day book and found the column marked 'religion' and began to jot down names. 'Benson and Butcher – C of E, Howden, West and Gentry – the same; Oldfield twins – Jehovah's witnesses.' He tutted loudly. 'Ah, here we are. O'Malley, Jensen, Thomas, Timmins, Dinfield twins, Lomas, and Kennett – and Ball. That seems to be the…' A loud siren sounded from the ward on the left to signal a medical emergency. I turned and ran, leaving him to his blessed list of children worthy of attention.

In the ward, a steam tent had been partially ripped away from a bed on which lay a small boy, his lips blue and he wasn't breathing. 'Respiratory arrest,' I said urgently to the junior nurse as I dropped the bedhead, pulling the tent further away still. 'Trevor!' I yelled. 'Call 222. Say Princess Margaret Ward and ask for the crash team, then come back here. We need everyone.' Sister Jenkins from a nearby ward arrived with two more nurses dragging an oxygen cylinder. I already had a mask on the child's face giving air whilst the oxygen was connected. Sister started cardiac massage and we went into a well-practiced routine. I was aware of Trevor beside me and he'd taken the boy's limp hand and with watery eyes was praying softly. We worked for what seemed like an age – only minutes in reality – until the crash team arrived with advanced life support equipment.

'Pulse?' asked Graham West, the senior paediatric registrar, placing his stethoscope on the little chest.

'One hundred and ten,' said Sister calmly, 'but still no

respiratory effort.'

Father Flynn appeared at the foot of the bed glowering, as Trevor prayed over the child. 'Reverend Evershall,' he shouted. 'That boy is Catholic. Now let me through.'

'This is not the time, Father,' said Sister, her voice even, though firm.

'But he's Catholic. It's inappropriate and I *must* give last rites.'

I gave the black-clad figure a withering stare.

'Sister,' said Graham West, 'his lungs are full of fluid. Get me a couple of 50ml syringes and the biggest needle you can find.'

'I'll go,' I said. The team's anaesthetist arrived, took over the boy's airway and he was connected to the Boyles machine that breathed for him. After grabbing what I needed I raced back to the bedside. 'Watch that, everyone,' I said indicating the floor, 'and don't slip.'

Little Geoffrey Makin had managed to divest himself of his nappy leaving a pile of poo on the floor. Graham West felt the boy's chest with expertise, then plunged the needle up to the hilt between the ribs and quickly withdrew 50ml of straw-coloured fluid. He repeated the action on the other side. The child gasped and spluttering, started to breathe to audible sighs of relief. His lips were now pink and he opened his eyes.

'Okay,' said Graham, 'let's get him to Intensive Care. All hands on deck.' The crisis was over. I turned. Transfixed, where the bottom of the bed had been, stood Father Flynn clutching Trevor by the arm.

'Are you all right, Father?' I ventured. His face was very pale.

'Jaysus, Nurse, I believe I have just witnessed a miracle.'

I watched as a ball of white light danced around his head. *Oh, no please!* I thought. For the past few months I'd been seeing lights just before someone died. I felt the colour drain from my face as Father Flynn finally let go of Trevor and shook himself back into action. 'I'd better go and see that wee Catholic boy in Intensive Care, if you'll excuse me.'

'Father, I made a mistake.' I called after him. 'In my haste to compile your list, I'm afraid I...he wasn't one of yours. I looked at the wrong line. He's a Jehovah's Witness, so your petty feud really doesn't matter now, does it?'

He looked horrified. Whether it was due to the solemnity of

the occasion or the fact that he'd nearly given the last rites to a non-Catholic, I don't know. His look turned to one of ill-disguised anger as he strode away without another word. But after only a few steps slipped on the pile of faeces that had escaped from little Geoffrey's nappy and shot along the ward like an ice skater with arms flailing, windmill style. Losing his glasses, he finally crashed into the tea trolley and lay very still.

'No, not here,' I cried. 'Not after slipping on a heap of shit – this cannot be happening.' I ran towards him and turned him over looking for signs of life, heaving a sigh of relief when he began to struggle to his feet, cassock covered in effluent. Trevor and I managed somehow to right him and my last glance was of him tottering down the corridor with everyone giving him a wide berth. A small, bright light continued to dance around his head and shoulders, and I feared he would soon need a miracle of his own.

Chapter 14

'Trevor, are you feeling okay?' I was passing the chapel late one evening on my way from the ward to the nurses' home. He was bending over a chair near the altar, his head on his chest. 'Well, no actually. I've had this niggling pain in my side for a few days now and it seems to be getting worse. Right here.' He put his hand just above his groin on the right side of his lower abdomen. 'It seems to come in waves and, to tell you the truth, Paola, I feel sick. I keep taking a couple of painkillers, but it's not made any difference today.' He winced again.

'Perhaps you should get it checked out. Nip into Casualty and let Sir Ivor have a look at you, just to be on the safe side.'

'Oh, I don't think it can be anything much – something I ate, I expect. I went over to Litton yesterday and had a long walk through the countryside. I probably pulled a muscle.'

'You went to see your friend?'

'My Becky,' he added, sitting on the front pew and stretching out his legs. 'Can you keep a secret?'

'You know I can, otherwise you wouldn't be asking,' I said, with an indulgent smile.

'You've become my confidante, Paola, and the first person I met when I came here.'

'You looked petrified, as I recall.'

'I was.' He shuffled uncomfortably on the hard seat and I sat down beside him. 'I've been trying to find the words to ask Becky to marry me, but each time I rehearse it...well, it just keeps coming out all wrong, ham-fisted and twee.'

'Then don't rehearse it, Trevor. Just blurt it out the next time it feels right.'

'Do you think so?'

'If you wait for the perfect time, you'll never get around to it, because that moonlight and roses moment may never come.' I closed my eyes and gestured to set the scene: 'The sun on the ocean about to disappear below the horizon and the smell of mimosa. Becky dressed in a beautiful flowing gown and you in your evening suit.' I smirked. 'Ask her when she's mucking out the sheep pens.'

He grinned. 'Oh, Paola, you *do* make me laugh.'

'Well if she loves you, she'll say 'Yes' whatever. Do you love her?'

'Aaaah,' he sighed, 'more than life itself.'

'And does she love you?'

'I've never asked her.'

'What...never?'

'Well, not in so many words.'

'Have you actually kissed her?'

'Yes, of course, many times.'

'Have you...'

'Certainly not! Her father has a very large pitchfork.' He pursed his lips and turned to me. 'Being a vicar's wife is certainly no country picnic.'

'Real life never is, Trev.'

'Aaagggh.' Suddenly, he leaned forward as another wave of pain swept over him. I felt his pulse to find it racing and he was sweating profusely.

That made up my mind. 'Trevor, sit there and don't move. I'm going to fetch a wheelchair.' He didn't argue. Pushing the chair, I ran to Casualty and threw open the blue swing doors to be confronted by Sir Ivor. I was never so glad to see him. 'Sir,' I began, 'it's Reverend Evershall. He's very ill.'

'I can see that, girl,' he barked, bending to look at Trevor. 'Push him into my room and then come and help me get his clothes off.'

'I'm sorry about this, Trevor,' I said, fumbling with his trouser buttons beneath a strategically placed modesty sheet.

'Hurry up, Nurse, and get a set of observations done,' ordered Sir Ivor.

I recorded his vital signs. 'Temperature 38.4, pulse 132/minute and blood pressure 90/60.'

'Pants off and get him on his side, Nurse.'

I helped a rather alarmed Trevor. 'I'm so sorry,' I said quietly, 'this must be really embarrassing.'

'Oh, get him undressed for God's sake and stop behaving like a vestal virgin,' barked Sir Ivor, with an irritated roll of his eyes. 'This man is *very* ill.'

I could see that.

'I'm going to do a rectal examination,' he announced to no one in particular, putting on a pair of rubber gloves. 'Lubrication, Nurse.' Trevor looked terrified, his eyes wide at the sight of the paw-like, gloved hands advancing on his nether regions.

'It's all right, Trevor, just concentrate on me. Squeeze my hand.' Sir Ivor looked over his glasses, raised his eyes to heaven and began. Trevor gave an almighty shriek.

'Right, young man,' announced Sir Ivor, 'you have a burst appendix. I need to operate immediately. There's fluid loose in your abdomen and that's not good. It's the knife for you, I'm afraid. Sign this consent form.' He turned to me. 'Get him ready, Nurse. There's not a moment to lose.'

I stood beside Trevor as he lay on the trolley in the anaesthetic room. 'Do you want me to contact Becky?' I asked.

'Oh, yes please.' He reeled off the number between gasps of pain. I wrote it on the inside of my wrist in biro as we waited for the anaesthetist to get changed and come to put him to sleep. 'Paola?' he whispered.

'Yes, mate...what is it?'

He gripped my hand. 'I know this makes me sound like a wimp, but I'm *really* scared.'

'It makes you sound nothing of the kind, but you're in good hands.'

'But, Paola, I have to tell you something.' He took a deep, painful breath. 'I *see* things.'

'What things?'

'I see, *and* I hear things – always have. Things I shouldn't believe in.'

I smiled, my face close to his ear. 'Like the light around Father Flynn?'

He looked at me strangely. 'And dead people that according to the teachings of the church aren't supposed to be there.'

'It's okay, Trevor...I see and hear them too.'

His eyes widened as he took it in. 'So, I'm not going mad?'

'Far from it. It's a gift. Well, that's what a good friend once told me. Try to accept it as such.' There was movement in the adjoining room that signalled the arrival of the anaesthetist.

'Paola, wait, before you go, answer me one thing truthfully?' He swallowed hard. 'Do you see any lights around me?'

I gave a small laugh and looked him straight in the eye. 'No Trev, you're as dull as bloody dishwater. Now go to sleep.' The anaesthetic team came in and with a last squeeze of his hand I went to phone Becky.

We'd got Trevor to theatre not a moment too soon. He had indeed a burst appendix that had spilled faecal matter into his abdominal cavity. This is serious because it contains hydrochloric acid secreted by the stomach as part of the digestive process. It not only burns, but releases poisons into the abdomen where they shouldn't be, causing peritonitis – a life-threatening condition.

It had taken Sir Ivor two hours to remove what was left of the appendix and flush out all the other material from Trevor's abdominal cavity. It was well after midnight when he was transferred to the recovery room – a high dependency area, where he could be carefully monitored.

About lunch time the following day I caught up with him on the surgical ward. He was in a single room, though not because he was dangerously ill. It was a courtesy to staff and we were good at looking after our own. He lay in bed, face pale against the snow-white linen, drips attached to both arms and with his wound drainage bottle hanging from the cot side rail. Beside him sat a stunningly beautiful young woman, her hand resting gently over his pale one. Long, dark curls cascaded down her back and her green eyes were damp with tears.

'Hello, Becky,' I whispered, so as not to disturb Trevor. 'We spoke on the phone.'

'Oh, Paola…' she stood to embrace me. 'I was so frightened I was going to lose him. I came as soon as you called, and when he came out of theatre, he looked more dead than alive.' Her lip trembled, and fresh tears fell.

'He's not going to die, Becky,' I said, my arm around her waist.

'He's far too much to do yet.'

Trevor stirred. I wet a flannel and wiped his face and he opened his eyes. 'Paola?' His voice was still thick from the anaesthetic.

'What, no dog collar, Rev? You won't be needing that for a few weeks.'

'No, perhaps not.' He tried to lick his dry lips.

'Drink?' He nodded. 'Just a sip or two, for now. Everything has to learn to work properly again after your adventure.' I held the cup as he wet his lips.

'We're going on another adventure, aren't we Trevor?' said Becky softly, her cheek against his hand. 'The greatest of all adventures.'

'Oh,' I said, raising my brows in anticipation.

'After the operation,' she continued, 'he opened his eyes and said, 'Marry me, Becky' and before I could answer he'd dropped off to sleep again. The next time he woke he was more compos mentis, but I wasn't sure he'd remember what he said. So, I took his hand and asked if he remembered asking me a question. He nodded and said, 'Well?' I told him the answer was 'Yes.' Then, he was asleep again.'

'I'm so happy for the pair of you,' I said. 'Congratulations and don't forget my invitation.'

The vicar and the sheep farmer's daughter were betrothed, but at that moment neither looked much like celebrating. What I saw though, was a blissfully happy couple about to embark on the greatest journey of their lives.

What Trevor didn't need to know, at least until he was stronger, was Father Flynn had died from a massive heart attack earlier that day. I wondered what had always made him seem so gloomy and unhappy. I'd always believed that faith was meant to be a joyous thing. Who can say what goes on in people's minds and makes them the way they appear? I hoped he'd found his peace, tranquillity, and lightness of mind, wherever he was, and that he was happier than he appeared before that life-light had finally gone out.

Chapter 15

'Pao, do you get seasick?' Shelagh asked after we'd stowed our luggage. We were climbing the staircase to the upper deck of the Liverpool to Dublin ferry.

'Not so far,' I said, 'but then again, you don't get very big waves on the lake in Queen's Park. I've only ever been on the Isle of Wight ferry and that was usually calm. Why do you ask?'

'Because the Irish Sea can get a bit rough at times. Legend has it that the gods of the sea did it on purpose to stop the Irish escapin' and the bloody English from invadin' our green land.'

I laughed. Ireland is steeped in folklore and superstition and Shelagh never tired of telling the tales of her home she referred to as 'the magical place'. She smacked her lips. 'Do yer fancy lunch then?'

We headed for the restaurant, which was a bit of a grand name for the small café on board, though it did afford wonderful views of the ocean. Shelagh had already polished off one cheese and ham roll and was about to lay into another. We'd been under way for about ten minutes and the ship had begun to pitch and roll. Pushing aside my sandwich, I stared into my coffee cup; the ripples mirrored the movement of the ship.

'Looks like we may be heading into a storm,' said Shelagh with a look at the darkening sky. 'Nothing new in that on this stretch of water, I'm afraid. The Irish Sea is notorious for it.'

'Really?' I said, swallowing, my gaze still fixed on the coffee's surface. I tore my eyes away. 'Shelagh, I think I'll go up on deck for a while to get a bit of fresh air. Valiantly, I tried to ignore my stomach which was complaining noisily.

'Aren't you eating yours, Pao? Because if you're not…?'

'Help yourself.' I indicated the food with a wave of my hand, wondering how she was managing to eat when the floor refused to keep still. Up on deck, I allowed the wind to blow unimpeded through my hair whilst trying to breathe slowly and fighting waves of nausea. I clutched at the ship's rail wishing I was on dry land, but there was none visible in any direction.

After a while, Shelagh appeared at my side. 'Bloody hell, Pao...you look terrible.'

'Thanks,' I said.

'You know what they say about seasickness?'

'Surprise me.' I tried not to retch.

'They do say that for the first hour you're afraid you might die and for the second hour, you're afraid you might not.'

'Oh, that's reassuring,' I said with ill-disguised sarcasm.

'The best thing to do is to come inside, sit down and fix your eyes on something stationary.

'Okay then.' I grabbed her arm. 'I'll try it. Is there anything stationary?'

'Probably not.'

'Got any brighter ideas?'

'Dunno, Pao. It's only what I've been told. I never had seasickness meself.'

'Then just leave me here to die by myself,' I said, taking hold of the rail again and closing my eyes.

And, something worked. Presently, I went back inside and slept soundly and when I woke we were docking in Dublin, very grateful to stand on firm ground again nevertheless. I thought of all those people who bend and kiss the ground on landing. They'd probably been seasick. By the time we boarded the train across Ireland, I felt much better and even managed a bowl of soup and a roll.

We passed through wonderfully green countryside, and after a few miles I felt I knew what 40 shades of green really meant. Alongside the tracks, contented cows gave us scant attention, busy with the task of chewing the cud.

'What a beautiful country you come from, Shelagh,' I remarked.

'Speaking of beauty,' said Shelagh, 'I've been meaning to tell you, so I have.'

I turned from the window to give her my full attention.

'You see...it's about our Declan...'

I thought we'd done well. He'd hardly been mentioned since

we'd boarded the ferry in Liverpool. 'Don't tell me,' I began. 'He's got a wooden leg?'

'Not exactly.'

My eyes widened in amusement. 'What then…? Out with it.'

'Well, you see…'

'Go on then, spit it out.'

'Now, let me see…how can I put this?'

I gave her a threatening look. 'Shelagh! Get to the flipping point.'

'Well, Pao, you know how some of us are blessed and some are not quite so blessed?'

'Yes. Tell me or else I'm going to scream.'

'Oh, please don't do that, Pao,' she said seriously, as I gave her a look that threatened imminent violence. 'Our Declan…let's just say he was towards the back of the queue when looks were given out, so he was.'

'And what does that mean?' I demanded, spitting out the words in exasperation.

'I'll try to put it as kindly as I can. Our Declan not only fell out of the ugly tree, but he hit every branch on the way down, so he did – the poor wee boy.'

I couldn't help myself and roared with uncontrollable laughter, falling sideways on the seat clutching my stomach, tears rolling down my cheeks.

'He can't help it, Pao – honest.' Her serious expression only made me worse. So, this was the man she'd been trying to palm me off with. At best, Quasimodo, and at worst, a short gargoyle! How bad could it get?

The train meandered its way across the Irish countryside. It was now bucketing down with rain. Now I knew the reason for its greenery. It lashed down for the rest of the journey, but the moment we pulled in to Sligo, the moon came out as if to herald our arrival and the air was beginning to cool.

The old stone farmhouse still shimmered in the twilight as we walked up the drive pulling our cases and suddenly we were surrounded by people.

'Fáilte, fáilte, girls. Welcome.' Shelagh's mother, Astrid, was a tall, elegant woman, not at all what I expected of a farmer's wife. Her hair was the deepest red and sculpted into a bob that came just below her ear lobes. Her nails were flawlessly polished in green, tapering long slim fingers that would have graced the keys of any pianoforte. But, the most striking feature about Shelagh's mother – or Ma, as she preferred to be called – were her eyes, large and beautiful, the colour of cut emeralds. She was a striking woman who, even in her late 40s would not have been out of place on a Paris catwalk. It was hard to image her mucking out the horses or chucking corn down for the chickens, though she did those things and more. Shelagh yawned.

'I expect you two would like to get to your beds early after travelling all day. I've made soda bread toast and there's a pot of chocolate keeping warm on top of the range. Paola, dear, you are now one of our considerably large family, so I beg you don't wait to be asked. Help yourself to whatever you want. We have no yours and mine here and you are welcome. As we say here, Fáilte. That word covers everything. Call me Astrid or Ma, whichever suits your fancy.'

Settling by the fire, we ate and drank then climbed the stairs to the second floor. Shelagh was in her old room that had been kept unchanged since the day she'd left it. My room was opposite hers and I was less concerned with looking around than sinking into the huge feather bed with its chintzy covers of cream and pink. Weary from the long journey, sleep came almost as soon as my head touched the soft pillow.

I awoke to a gentle knock on the bedroom door. Astrid had brought mugs of steaming coffee and Shelagh decamped into my room. She stretched out on my bed like a contented cat. 'I'm home, Pao. It feels wonderful.' Warm sun streamed in through the window as I drew back the curtains to let in the new day. Wherever you go in the world, the smell of the countryside is instantly recognisable. It's the smell of green fields, wild flowers, and pure, clean air. And somewhere there was bacon frying.

We dressed quickly and went down to the huge farm kitchen I'd barely noticed the night before being so very weary. In the centre of the room was a huge pine table set for breakfast that was being prepared by Shelagh's father, Eoghan. He turned as we entered, spatula in hand to greet us.

'Fáilte, Paola…and my darling girl.'

Shelagh embraced him. 'Oh, Da, I've missed you so.'

Now this was more what I expected a farmer to look like: large of girth with a weathered complexion from working outside in all weathers. He'd been up at five for the milking, and that completed, had set about cooking breakfast for the whole family. It was the tradition in the household I was later told. Laying down his spatula, he moved to the door and opened it to yell upstairs. 'Dan…Siobhan…Cass…Jonny…Declan…the food is on the table – and be sure to button yer pants. We have a guest.' The sound of pairs of feet coming downstairs heralded the arrival of hungry children. First came Danny, 14 and still a bit awkward and gawky; Siobhan and Cassandra, twins, aged eight, tall and willowy for their age, blessed with their mother's red hair, wildly curly after the night. Jonny at 18 held out his hand to shake mine; such a good-looking boy with dark close curls and the complexion of his father. And last came Declan.

'You must be Miss Paola Green,' he said, also offering his hand for me to shake.

Well, I thought, *Shelagh wasn't exaggerating*. He was quite short and not what you'd call easy on the eye. He had large protruding ears and rather prominent teeth. But he had the most enchanting smile that set his green eyes twinkling and lit up his face, so you forgot everything else.

'I'm very pleased to meet you all at last,' I said. 'I've heard an awful lot about you these past three years.' The twins began to bombard me with questions, moving to sit one on either side, so it resembled a game of tennis. What was England like? Was it difficult to be a nurse? Did some of the patients smell funny?'

'Now girls,' said Astrid waving her hand, 'you will leave Paola alone this second. There'll be plenty of time to talk after breakfast *and* the washing up. She included the boys in a sweeping gesture. 'And I do mean *everyone*. Now eat.'

'Yes, Ma,' came a collective petulant grumble at the very thought of chores.

I'd never seen the like of what was laid out before us. There was bacon, eggs, black pudding, mushrooms, oatcakes and tomatoes by the bowlful. Then came sizzling, fried potatoes and mountains of hot buttered toast, and kippers to be washed down with huge mugs of tea. Breakfast was clearly the most important meal of the day. On a farm, hard labour required fuelling and a good start was probably essential. I ate more than I'd ever eaten at breakfast in my life and when we were all truly sated, I sat back.

'Will yer have a bit more bacon, Paola?' asked Eoghan, 'or perhaps a kipper?'

'No thanks, I couldn't eat another thing,' I said. 'That was wonderful, but I won't need to eat for another three days now.' They all laughed.

'Nonsense,' he replied, 'there's room on the pair of you. You're both too thin. I don't know what they've been feeding you in that hospital, but it's not enough. Never mind, we'll soon put that to rights, so we will.'

I wondered whether my uniforms would still fit when I got home. I rose to help clear away. Astrid, held up her hands.

'No, I will not hear of it. You two can go off and enjoy yourselves. The boys can wash up today, can't you boys?' There were a few more grunts and grumbles. 'Now, step lively the three of you. Da has to go to the village and then there's the cows to feed, eggs to collect and the chickens and ducks need fresh bedding and, *when* you've finished that,' she went on hardly pausing for breath, 'the bottom gate and a bit of the fence needs mending.'

There were sounds of resignation. 'Yes, Ma,' as they began to clear away the dishes.

Shelagh said she was going to show me the nearby village that led down to the sea, where, according to legend, the leprechauns lived in a cave on the beach. 'Da…we'll be going now,' she called over her shoulder.

He grinned. 'Now don't you be forgettin' to take a gift to please the little people,' he said, handing her a foil-wrapped parcel.'

'Thanks, Da.'

'Shelagh, what is that?' I asked as we walked down the path that led across green fields to the beach.

'Oh, 'tis only cake. We need to bribe them a little, you see.'

'Bribe who…the fairies?'

'They're called leprechauns, Pao – sprites, wee folk.'

120

'Shelagh,' I said, giving her a smile of indulgence, 'do you *really* believe in all this? I mean, *really?*'

'Why, of course I do!' She turned to me with a deadly serious look on her face. 'You disbelieve at your peril, so you do. You must keep them happy when you visit them, or the hens won't lay, the cows' milk won't be rich and good and...'

'Doesn't that come from the green grass and all that flipping rain?' I interrupted.

Shelagh wagged her finger at me. 'Paola Green...don't you dare mock. Do I make fun of you, or disbelieve in *your* voices? Why is it different from hearing and seeing someone who's supposed to be dead? Let me tell you, if I were to see the things you do, I'd shit meself proper, so I would.'

I bit my bottom lip thoughtfully. I suppose there really was little difference. 'Okay, then, so where do we leave this cake?'

We climbed down the hillside leading to the ocean with its pretty sandy coves bordered with tough sea grasses and pink thrift. I breathed in the warm salty air and knew instantly that I loved this land. There's something about Ireland that takes you over and wheedles its way into your soul. For it *is* a magical place that lends itself to mystery and folklore; making it easy to seduce you into a belief in myths and legends almost without you realising.

The coast possesses its own strange light, sometimes ethereal, in the way the mist hangs down like a thin curtain over the sea, nearly transparent and silent except for birdsong in the uncluttered morning air. And, an equally strange peace comes along with it. I suddenly understood how 'The Lark Ascending' came to be written on such a day as this and found new meaning in the piece of music from that moment. I think Shelagh saw that sentiment on my face, as she stayed quiet as I mused, before I broke my own reverie with one word. 'Beautiful,' I said, breathlessly.

We walked down a small sandy incline to the beach, through the dunes, bordered on either side by sea holly and clumps of dense grey-green tufts of marram grass. Leaving our walking shoes and socks beyond the reach of the tide, we ran to dabble our feet in the surf at the water's edge. I gasped at the water's icy coldness, which was eye-watering, 'Oh, good grief, Shelagh, it's absolutely freezing, and it's supposed to be summer. Does it *ever* warm up?'

Shelagh laughed and shook her head. ''Tis the Atlantic Ocean, so it is. It may get a few degrees higher in mid-summer, but that's your lot! You have to be a hardy soul to go surfin' here and the waves can get pretty high sometimes, Pao. The leppie's cave is often underwater. You really have to know the tides if you're goin' to swim here. It might look inviting but there's a huge rip that goes right to left that can take the strongest swimmer unawares. More than a few have died here in the past.'

I looked out over the benign-looking sea. It was hard to imagine with tiny waves hardly breaking on the shore today. I said nothing as the fine hairs on the back of my neck began to rise and prickle – and suddenly, I felt them. Shelagh was still dipping her toes in the water a little further away, a light breeze blowing her long, auburn hair behind her – not with the same intensity of colour as her mother's, though beautiful nevertheless.

They spoke to me, those lost souls and I saw them clearly; a man carrying a child of no more than eight, just a small boy held in his father's arms. Another boy lay on the sand by the tide line, seaweed draped across his features and in his hair. A young man knelt by his side and brushed the green strands from his lifeless face. He looked towards me, pleading.

I tried to save him…really, I did. Father will be so angry. I tried my best. You see, I was supposed to be looking after him. Although the young man's lips hadn't moved, I listened as his voice invaded my mind. He looked no more than sixteen himself.

'It's all right,' I whispered, my eyes locked on his. 'Your father forgave you. Be still now.'

He turned back to his brother and, lifting him up into his arms, began to walk towards the sea and they both faded from sight as a cacophony of cries surrounded me. The sound became weaker and weaker, until only the whisper of the wind remained.

'Paola, look, there's the cave.' Shaking myself back to the present, I followed Shelagh a little way along the beach and there it was, its mouth yawning greedily. We went in through the damp, lichen-coated, rocky walls dripping with water that in a few thousand years would probably turn into stalactites. I grinned, remembering my grandfather's joke, 'You see, young lady, tites always come down!' There'd always been a mischievous look in his eye no matter how many times he said it. My mother had elbowed him in the ribs and told him not to be so rude in front of the children.

Shelagh placed a finger to her lips to ask for quiet as, reverentially, she unwrapped the cake pieces and walked a little further into the cave to place them onto a flat area of rock. It looked like a green-coated altar. I watched, a little bemused, but why not pay homage to the god of the sea who had taken as well as given? Why not appease the water sprites, whether you believed or not? Did it matter? Someone had been there before us to place lighted candles alongside the altar stone, so the little people that protected this place might eat in comfort.

As I turned away to leave, I saw a small girl cowering and clinging to the edge of the feasting table. She held a ragged, dripping toy donkey. Wet, baby curls of hair framed her pale, waxen face. 'Mama,' she whimpered, 'Mama, where are you?' Her saucer-like blue eyes bore into mine. 'Mama told me to hold on, but I let go of her hand, I did!'

I shivered and closed my eyes for a moment. Shelagh had already walked from the cave. I knelt to the child's level. 'Walk to the light, little one. Walk into the light,' I told her softly. 'Mama is waiting for you there in the light. Go now, little one.' Her trusting baby eyes were soft. She turned away and, still clutching her donkey, walked through the solid cave wall and was gone.

We had brought our gift and acknowledged their existence, so we left them in peace, protected from the cool winds and the salty air.

'Oh, will yer come on, Pao,' called Shelagh from outside. 'Don't be dawdlin' because the little people aren't about to feast with the both of us here.'

I glanced back into the darkest recesses of the cave, beyond the little candle-lit altar. Shelagh was right. There *were* little people here; the custodians of the dead souls who had perished on this stretch of shoreline – so peaceful today, so benignly beautiful. They remained here in the sanctuary of this place. I took a deep breath and gently blew out warmed air and left them to their eternity.

'Will yer come on, Pao,' Shelagh yelled, louder this time. 'The tide's rising fast. Hurry up!'

I was astounded to see waves already lapping at the mouth of the cave. It would soon be flooded, the altar candles extinguished, and nature would reclaim it again until the tide turned once more. The wind had picked up with the incoming sea by the time we reached the path that led to the beach where our shoes and socks awaited our return. We sat, side by side, on a soft carpet of sand and scrubby grass, pausing to dust our feet.

'Shelagh, I can't believe how quickly the tide comes in,' I said, fastening my shoes. Angry spume-topped waves were now biting hungrily at the sand just below where we sat.

'Some say that when it turns, it comes in faster than a galloping horse,' said Shelagh, 'and many a person's been caught out like that, I can tell yer. You're in big trouble if yer stay too long in the cave. It's hard to outrun a fast tide like that.'

A sudden gust of cold wind whipped at our skin and hair, lashing us with stinging grains of sand. Shelagh looked up at the sky, until a few moments ago, clear and blue. Now, as if from nowhere, grey thunderhead clouds were rolling in from the vast expanse of ocean to the west. Shelagh stood and stared over the horizon, her skirts blowing. 'A storm's coming. Can you smell it, Pao?'

'No, can't say I can.' I shivered, goose bumps rising on my arms as the sun disappeared behind a cloud.

'May God protect the souls on the sea,' said Shelagh, 'and keep them safe.'

'Amen to that,' I replied as we began to hurry back the way we had come. It would have to wait until the storm had cleared before she took me to see the wild coast of Sligo which lay to the other side of the village. It was the part she'd always waxed so lyrical about, but now large droplets of rain were beginning to fall. So, holding cardigans over our heads, we made for the tearooms and shelter.

'Shelagh,' I asked tentatively, as we sat sipping coffee by the window, 'do you ever have any trouble here?'

'Oh, just the odd bit of petty pilfering – just kids mainly. Nothing better to do than get into mischief, I expect.'

'No,' I said, '*the* Troubles.'

'Oh, *that!*' She sighed deeply. 'There've been rumours, of course, but nothing like up north. We don't talk about it much. Whether Ma and Da do when they're alone, I can't say, but it's not favoured conversation around the dinner table.' She paused to drain her cup. 'You see, a distant cousin – I'm sure I must have told you this, Pao – a terrible miscarriage of justice, so it was!'

'You told me a few times and...' But it was too late to stop her now and she was off. And on it went for five full minutes with barely a pause for breath. There was no point trying to cut it short. The tirade, as usual, must run its course.

'Sweet boy,' she added as an afterthought, 'couldn't even blow up a paper bag, *and* may I say, not enough brains to be even thinking about any such thing either. He just got in with the wrong crowd and still another year to go in Armagh jail, so he has.'

'Perhaps he'll get some time knocked off for good behaviour...' I ventured.

'Let's hope so. He was always such a good catholic boy. Broke his mother's heart, so it did. What the hell he was doin' with them nutters from over the border...well, Himself only knows.' There was no stopping her, so I sat back and resigned myself to another ten minutes of it. I let her rant on to the otherwise empty café, even though I'd heard it many times before.

It was my own fault. I shouldn't have brought the subject up. *Next time, Paola Green, take your foot out of your mouth and shut up.* I admonished myself silently as the finale approached and Shelagh threw up her arms in righteous indignation and took a breath at last.

I felt responsible. 'Sorry, Shelagh, I shouldn't have brought it up.'

'No, it's me who should apologise. I'm sorry, Pao, were you perhaps wondering if you'd be safe here...with you not being a Catholic and all?'

'Actually,' I said, 'I never gave it a thought.'

She put her hand lightly on my shoulder. 'You are safe. We're not savages you know, and my brothers would willingly lay down their own lives for their women, so they would.'

I was about to reply that I *wasn't* one of their women but

thought the better of it, opting for silence instead, but deciding to make a point of not standing out from the crowd, just in case.

Chapter 16

'Are you of a mind to take a small walk, Paola?'

'Sorry…?' I looked up from my book where I'd been reading, sitting in the window seat after another huge breakfast. The sun was streaming through the window and Shelagh was upstairs taking a bath. She was singing loudly and could clearly be heard.

'When I was a lad about 18 or so, with me books and me pencils to school I did go…' She could really belt out a tune that girl, and the reason I hadn't heard Declan come in. Now he stood in the doorway, reminding me of one of Tolkien's hobbits: very short with impossibly large feet. I laid down my book.

'Declan,' I said affably, 'hello again.'

'Paola, would you care to take a walk and come and see me pigs?' He looked less than certain I'd come, and as a chat-up line, it was unique.

I smiled broadly and stood up from the window seat. 'I'd absolutely love to; just let me change out of these slippers.'

His face lit up with ill-disguised surprise and pleasure, bushy eyebrows almost meeting his hairline. He hopped from foot to foot with glee. 'Then you'd better borrow Siobhan's wellies,' he said. 'It can get a bit chewed up down the field and I bet they'll fit you.' His eyes hadn't left my face, probably looking for signs I was about to change my mind.

'Are you sure?'

He studied my feet for a second. 'Oh yes, they'll fit.' He briefly disappeared, returning a few moments later with his eight-year-old sister's wellington boots – and they did fit. My size two feet had never anchored me well in a storm. I was amazed that any man would be so observant as to notice something as mundane as the size of my feet.

We walked side by side through the garden that was clearly someone's pride and joy. Judging by the length of Astrid's fingernails I couldn't have imagined that she was the one responsible for not one weed being visible in the flowerbed, unless she wore extremely stout gardening gloves.

'Ma's patch,' said Declan, putting an end to my wondering. 'Isn't it glorious? Real green fingers she has.' He grinned broadly displaying a set of very large white teeth below the mantelpiece of his upper lip.

The tall delphiniums were coming to the end of their display, but the yellow, blowsy blooms of the old-fashioned roses were still resplendent, each fading bloom having been removed to make way for the next.

Declan paused to tuck his trouser bottoms into his sturdy working boots. Even in the heat of the summer days he still wore a jerkin, looking the part of a true farmer's boy. As he bent, the sun cast a shadow emphasising his protruding ears even more.

Oh my, Shelagh, I thought, *I sincerely hope you haven't given this boy any false expectations!* Declan stood a good two inches smaller than me but had a very muscular figure for his size.

'There now,' he said and straightened. 'Would you be knowing anything about pigs, Paola?'

'Only that they taste good with apple and onion sauce,' I said, my eyes twinkling back at him.

'Well, that's a start then.'

We laughed, and to my surprise, I found I was completely at ease in the company of this strange little fellow with the ruddy complexion whose face told the story of an outdoor life with all its harsh realities. But today, with the sun shining down giving late summer warmth, all that seemed far off as we walked through the daisy-covered meadow that led to his one true love.

'Have you ever tasted clover, Paola?'

'As a matter of fact, I have,' I said.

Declan sat on the grass to pick a small bunch of red clover and began to take it apart, putting the petals between his lips to taste and handing me some. 'The red tastes completely different to the white,' he said between petals. ''Tis pure sugar you see, and when we feed it to the pigs, it sweetens their meat, so it does.'

For a few moments I became lost in thought, transported back to High Meadow, above the village where I was born. Sucking on a piece of clover, the years melted away as quickly as snow in June. I plonked myself down in the grass beside him. 'Let me tell you about one of the favourite places from my childhood,' I said, 'before we go and see the pigs.'

Declan lay beside me, supported on his elbows, listening and watching me whilst chewing on a piece of clover with those tombstone teeth of his. I told him I used to go there as a child, and then as a young adult, to lie among the grass and wildflowers, enjoying the solitude of my own company in a world that seemed much safer. And I'd watch the meadow browns and the blue heath butterflies as they flitted around collecting nectar. I told him this was *my* special place. What I didn't say was that it was the place I felt closest to Linnie, my long-dead friend. Or that it was where I'd seen her and tried to follow as she'd walked away from me, her auburn hair ruffling in the soft breeze as she passed beyond my gaze. I would not tell him that. I'd never told anyone since Robbie and it was my memory alone and not for sharing – not even with Shelagh.

'Hey, Mistress Paola...' His words shook me from the reverie of my daydream. 'I do believe you had gone off somewhere.' And, scrambling to his feet, he held out a hand. I took it and felt rough skin against my own as we walked on towards the piggery.

I gasped. 'Declan, they're beautiful. What breed are they?'

His eyes twinkled with the pride akin to a new father showing his latest offspring. He climbed the wall of the piggery and slid down into the pen where a large golden sow lay on her side, contentedly suckling eight very young piglets. They lay in near-perfect symmetry at right angles to their mother, snouts buried in her belly. 'Tammies,' he said softly, his eyes on the sow. 'Tamworths. We call them Irish grazer pigs. A very old breed they are.'

The only other pigs I'd seen were at a farm along the lane from where we grew up. They were a sort of mud-wallowed pink. And I called myself a country girl! Declan told me that despite being called Tamworths – a name that was adopted later – these were descended from the most ancient breed in Ireland.

As I watched in wonder, Declan bent to stroke the sow's

muzzle, and in reply she made a talkative, cooing sound clearly trusting him with her small babies. Nursing sows are not known for their tolerance of anyone invading the farrowing pen and can inflict a savage bite. I remember our local farmer warning us kids not to get too close. I looked at Declan and marvelled at his affinity with this animal that could easily have flattened him if she saw fit.

'Ah...this one's a good mother,' he said softly. 'Aren't you now, Flora?'

'You give them names?' I asked, raising my eyebrows.

'Why, of course.'

'But, how on earth can you give something a name and then eat it?' I asked.

He laughed. 'Oh, Flora here's not for the market. She's a breeder, so she is, and she's very good at it, aren't you Flora?' He continued to rub the sow's nose and she was clearly enjoying the attention.

This huge pig would have easily fed the entire village, but I could see that she was a far greater asset producing further stock. 'Will they spend their whole lives in the pen?' I asked.

'No,' said Declan. 'As soon as they're weaned, they'll be free to roam the fields, eating all the vegetable stalks, grains, and potato peelings, plus the silage we feed them. And they'll forage on windfall apples and bracken for the next six months.'

I sat on the wall listening to him, mesmerised. Without really trying, I was learning an awful lot about pigs.

A large stone hit the wall beneath, dislodging me from my perch and I slid into the farrowing pen. 'What the...?' I ducked down instinctively in the soft mud at the foot of the wall.

'Hey...pig boy!' It was a rough Irish voice. 'We see yer, pig boy. Get outta that pen, yer dirty little wanker. We know what yer be doin' in there, so we do...pulling yerself off an all.'

Declan had crawled over to me and placed his hand on my shoulder, gesturing that I should stay down and out of sight.

'What?' I mouthed, spreading my palms in a question.

Footsteps approached and the sound of laughter. Cruel, male, vindictive, throaty laughter. 'We know you're there, pig boy. Out yer come, now.' There was a pause. 'Well, let's see how yer like this then.' There was a sudden rattle as the swill bucket was lifted and seconds later, the entire contents were poured over the wall hitting Declan squarely but missing me, save for a few stray strands of potato peelings. I spat them away ferociously, anger rising. I looked at Declan. He had swill dripping from his hair and with an almighty shriek of horror I seized the two-pronged pitchfork propped in the corner of the sty and vaulted the wall in one leap. Anger and injustice have always had this effect on me.

Three scruffy teenage boys were taken completely off their guard and momentarily seemed rooted to the spot by the sudden appearance of a supposed crazy woman covered in peelings and howling like a banshee.

'Right, you bastards,' I spat, brandishing the pitchfork. 'Which one of you is getting it first, then?'

With cries of alarm, two of the lads peeled off and ran for the hedge, tripping and stumbling, more from shock than anything else, finally emerging from the brambles scratched and bleeding. The third boy was not so lucky. I lunged at this sallow youth with the pitchfork and he screamed, his face turning bright red. I lunged again my teeth bared like one of Boudicca's wronged warrior daughters. This time he was backed up against the wooden gate of the piggery, the two prongs of the pitchfork embedded in the wood either side of his neck. The expression of horror on his face told that any minute he believed he was about to meet his maker. He grasped at his neck, babbling incoherently.

'What the hell do you think you're playing at?' I demanded, still holding the handle firmly and giving him a swift kick on both shins for good measure.

He howled. 'Sorry, Missus. We didn't mean it, we didn't. We thought...'

I shrieked. 'You thought, you thought...you're not smart enough to think – any of you! Now get, before I skewer you like a kipper.' Finding extra strength from anger I yanked the fork out of the wood. 'And don't bloody well come back.'

He fled, at speed, into the brambles.

I fell to the ground exhausted but still with adrenaline pumping, breathing hard and still clutching the pitchfork.

Declan's head appeared over the wall. 'Oh, my God,' he whispered. 'I thought you were about to fuckin' kill them, so I did!' He tried to help me up from the muddy ground which was littered with pigswill and after several unsuccessful attempts we made it to our feet.

I grimaced. 'Who were *they?*'

'*They* were the Gillivers. Twins and a spare bully-boy brother.'

'Do they often treat you like that?'

'Oh, it's no matter, really.' He tapped the side of his large nose. 'One day... I'm just biding me time. One day when they least expect it, you'll see.' He bent to pick up the empty swill bucket, caught sight of me and burst out laughing.

'What...? What?' I was now laughing too.

Carefully, he took the pitchfork from me. Mud was caked on my clothes and hair. I had lost one welly boot and my other foot was sinking into the mud. For the first time, I took a good look at myself, then at Declan who was still liberally coated in pigswill. A strand of yellow cabbage was draped across his head and festooned down over one ear.

'My God, Declan O'Flaharty, you certainly know how to show a woman a good time.'

'And that, Paola Green, is one of the nicest things anyone has ever said to me, so it is.'

Guffawing with laughter and holding each other up we started to make our way home. Tears were making tracks down my cheeks through the grime and by the time we reached the house, flies were beginning to follow us attracted by the smell of rotting vegetation. The mud on my skin was setting like cement, my jeans becoming stiffer with each step. But something else was happening that had nothing to do with our present state, and that was the cementing of a true friendship.

I will never forget the horrified looks that greeted us at the kitchen door. We thought we'd better use the tradesmen's entrance given our current state of contamination. Shelagh and her parents stared open-mouthed as Declan tried to explain our hapless adventures. Astrid looked ready to strike him with the fish slice she was brandishing. Shelagh reached for a blanket. 'I'll run the bath, so I will,' was all she managed to say with her mouth set in a tight line of bewildered humour; ever the practical one, Shelagh.

Later, after soaking off what seemed like half a field, I returned to the kitchen. It had taken three tubs of water before the stolen earth of Sligo had finally gone down the plughole.

In that short time, I'd developed a certain notoriety. Declan had recounted our adventures with gusto, after he'd first dunked himself in the horse trough and then showered. He'd told how a tiny English woman had taken on the three Gilliver brothers single-handed and had damned near killed one of them. I thought it to be a bit of an exaggeration – but only just. Eoghan nodded sagely and said they were a 'bad lot'. I began to wonder if indeed we'd heard the last of them.

Chapter 17

'Have you ever been to a ceilidh, Pao? I mean a *real* one?' We were again seated at the table hardly able to move after another of Eoghan's breakfasts.

'No, I don't believe I have.'

'Then you haven't lived,' said Shelagh, suddenly animated. 'Oh, yer in for a treat then, so yer are. It's in the village hall next to the Black Bull, so there'll be no shortage of drink – and there's a great band.' After hearing about these events from Shelagh in the past, I was anxious to see a genuine, Irish folk band. 'It's a bit of a cheat really,' she continued, 'our Dec plays drums in the band, so we don't have to pay them. They're very good though and do it for the beer money.'

'And as you will have gathered by now, Paola,' said Eoghan, 'we Irish don't need much of an excuse for a party and a good sing-song. But, if you're expecting tea and sandwiches, you might want to think again. It's for the adults to enjoy themselves and not for kids.'

I'd only brought one decent outfit with me, a little black lace dress on the off-chance we went somewhere posh. This was going to be the opportunity to wear it as, so far, casual had been the order of the day. I was a bit fearful I may not be able to zip it up after a week of Eoghan's cooking. 'I was going to wear this, Shelagh?' I said later, holding up the dress. 'Do you think it will be okay? Is it too much?'

'I think you'll wow the place and I'm going to wear somethin' slinky meself. No point in going out and not making an impression, is there now?'

I'd grown my hair after years of wearing it short, even if it was much more trouble. I was tired of looking boyish. It now reached my shoulders and I had the choice to wear it up or down.

For work, it *always* had to be pinned up and hidden under the confines of a nurses' cap. Tonight, we could let our hair down – literally. We laid out our clothes on Shelagh's bed in preparation and, as rain was threatening, decided to stay around the house and make ourselves available for any chores, though Astrid wouldn't hear of it. So, we sat and read all afternoon.

'Paola, do you believe in ghosts?' I was completely taken by surprise at the question that came from one of the twins that evening.

'What on *earth* makes you ask that?' I said.

'Because our Shelagh says you do.' Siobhan and Cassandra sat on the floor side-by-side, cross-legged, indistinguishable from one another apart from the different coloured ribbons in their hair.

What should I say to a pair of eight-year-olds? After pondering for a moment, I thought it safest to answer a question with a question. 'Do you?' I asked, looking from one to the other.

'Our Dan says there aren't any such things, but...' said Cass.

'We think there *are*,' finished Siobhan. It was uncanny how they completed each other's sentences. 'What do *you* think, Paola?' they added in unison. They were not about to let me off the hook.

'I think there *are* such things,' I said gently, 'but they're usually very shy and only special people can see them.'

The girls looked at each other and nodded in agreement. Identical twins seem to have an instant connection. After all, they developed from the same egg and shared everything from the day of conception. 'Paola, can you keep a secret?'

Oh gosh, how many times had I been asked that? But I got the impression that this was a very different secret to the one the O'Flannagan boy had asked me to keep. On that occasion, I'd been unable to keep my promise. 'Of course, I can,' I lied with a smile, 'though the best secrets are the ones you can share with someone you love and trust...like your ma.'

They nodded in unison, hair ribbons bobbing. 'Do you believe in elves and fairies, Paola?' asked Cass with a serious expression.

'Well... I don't know. I've never actually seen any.'

'What...never?' Their eyes were wide as they looked at each

other again for unspoken confirmation and nodded.

'Would you *like* to see them, Paola?'

I hesitated as they continued to stare at me with those wide eyes. 'Well, yes. I suppose I would.'

They exchanged a look of triumph. 'We'll go tomorrow, after school. Will you come? Say you will, please Paola.'

I smiled. 'Okay then. I'll look forward to it.'

With that they jumped up and went to play.

I shook my head. *What are you doing, Paola Green?* I *would* go along with it, for childhood dreams should never be held up to ridicule. I would indulge any fantasy they had and if I needed to pretend, then what harm could it do? We grow up far too quickly and move on to a less appealing world where the realities of adulthood leave no room for such notions. There would be plenty of time for the girls to grow up.

The pair was waiting for me as soon as school was over. They'd changed into their play clothes and pumps. 'Ma says it's all right if we go walking with you, Paola,' said Cass, with a knowing look at her twin. 'But we must be back in for tea by five-thirty.'

'Come on, then,' I said, 'let's go.'

Each grabbed one of my hands as we walked. The August afternoon was warm and sunny as we strolled away from the house and down the lane to the edge of the trees. 'Where are we going, girls?' I asked.

'Why, to the fairy glen where the elves come out to play,' they chimed together. 'But they'll only come if we're very quiet,' whispered Siobhan, unexpectedly taking the lead. 'So, you'll have to walk *very* carefully.'

'Okay,' I whispered back, playing the game.

Quietly, we walked through the trees with only the odd snap of a twig underfoot to disturb the silence, the girls now leading. Presently, we came to a clearing. Shafts of late afternoon sun filtered through the branches overhead to the grassy middle where there was a fallen tree, its bark coated with bright moss.

'Are we there yet?' I asked reminiscent of a childhood car journey.

'This is the fairy glade,' whispered Siobhan, 'and if we are *very* quiet, the elves may come out to dance.'

'What do these elves look like?' I asked softly.

'You'll see,' they said in unison, as we sat on the edge of the soft, green area by the tree line, watching and waiting for whatever it was.

'Siobhan placed a finger to her lips. There was a faint rustling in the undergrowth. 'They're coming,' said her twin as a baby rabbit broke cover and hopped into the grassy arena. It paused to sniff the air as if detecting a new scent, then, satisfied there was no risk, began to nibble the lush grass. It was quickly joined by another six, all pausing to test the air in their turn.

'Can you see them, Paola?' whispered Cass.

'I see some lovely baby rabbits,' I said softly.

'No, Paola, look carefully. The elves are riding on their backs.'

Shafts of sunlight seemed to make the rabbits' soft fur sparkle as they fed, and dust motes danced in the warm air.

'Look, Paola,' said Cass. 'Can you see? *Now* the elves are dancing.' We sat in silence and I watched the girls carefully, their eyes wide with wonder. After all, I was an adult and not party to what they saw with such obvious delight. The children watched as the little men in their green coats danced in the fairy glade, their senses heightened by this magical place with its tall trees and pretty clearing. If elves and fairies existed, they would certainly have come here to dance. My adult eyes saw only seven baby rabbits feeding contentedly in the late afternoon, but who was I to destroy their fantasy?

A branch snapped with a loud crack somewhere in the woodland and startled, the rabbits disappeared into the undergrowth, no doubt still carrying their elfin riders.

The girls looked up at me. 'You saw them, Paola, didn't you?'

'I saw them,' I said. 'What a wonderful place.' And laughing, we walked quickly back through the trees.

Happy children. Whatever they saw, be it dust motes in sunlight or something conjured from their imagination, it didn't matter. It was real to them. If I had been eight years old, I might have been able to see the elves too. Saddened, I hankered after childhood once again, when all was fresh, new and believable, instead of the harsh realities of growing up in a world where there's little room for fantasy. The secret they had shared with me would be kept.

Chapter 18

We heard the music long before we reached the hall in the middle of the village. The building with its wavy, corrugated roof sat between the Black Bull and the butcher's shop. In fact, the window was shaking as a fiddler hammered out Irish dance music. A gipsy violin was being played to within an inch of its life, twangs of melody floating unimpeded through the early evening air.

'Paola, you came!' Declan spotted us the moment we walked through the door, rushing towards us across the fast-filling dance floor. It was as though the whole village had turned out, seduced by the prospect of a dance and a few pints of Guinness. Eoghan promptly disappeared into the pub next door and returned with a large tray of drinks.

'And now, Paola,' he said with a flourish of a bow, 'have you ever tasted our national drink?' He held up a pint glass with its creamy inch of head. 'The Guinness.'

'No,' I said, 'I'm strictly a G and T girl.'

'Well, my sweet English rose,' he began, 'this is your initiation, so it is. You can't come to Ireland without trying the black stuff.' A small crowd had gathered around the two of us, Eoghan with a mischievous glint in his eye. 'To our guest.' He raised the glass aloft and everyone else did the same and then he passed it to me. 'C'mon now. Fáilte!'

A chorus of the same broke out around me as they all began to clap, slowly at first, then faster and faster. There was no escape and I lifted the glass, took a deep breath, and drank. After the first shock of an unfamiliar taste, it went down with surprising ease. I drained the glass in one go to cheers, punching my fist in the air in triumph. I held the glass aloft and gave an unexpected loud burp to roars of laughter, and then everyone got on with the party. My initiation was over. I'd passed with flying colours and become accepted as a temporary Irish person. My G and T days were numbered because I've loved Guinness ever since.

A drum-beat struck up from the stage in the corner and everyone turned and began to gather round. Declan was playing his drum, the bodhran. Slowly the rhythm increased, his head bowed, eyes closed, oblivious to the room; his soul lost to the hypnotic tempo of the sound he played. The audience was rendered silent by Declan's playing, awestruck at the speed his hands moved over the instrument. Presently he was joined by a penny whistler, the crowd now clapping in time to the melody and the frantic beat of Declan's drum. The last two members of the band took to the stage; a fiddler and a fair-haired man carrying a folk guitar. My head swam a little from the quickly ingested Guinness. The music rose to a deafening crescendo and the crowd roared their approval, and with the song at an end, the four bowed to the audience.

Eoghan again disappeared to the Black Bull to refill the glasses. The rest of the family sat at a table near the stage. Declan joined us, downing his pint of Guinness in one gulp then gave me a toothy smile and a wink. 'Did yer know I could play, Paola?'

I told him that I'd no idea and I'd never even heard of a bodhran, let alone heard one played. 'Shelagh never mentioned it and with you being able to play so well too. It's a wonderful sound.'

He bent over to whisper in my ear. 'Paola, the Lord didn't give me the good looks and so I suppose he had to make up for it in other ways. I can make a passable attempt at most instruments.'

'Oh, Declan,' I said, 'don't do yourself down. But he didn't seem to mind the way he looked or maybe he was accustomed to hiding his feelings. The DJ put on a record, 'Honky Tonk Woman' by the Rolling Stones.

Declan gave a small bow and held out his hand. 'Miss Green, may I have the pleasure of this dance?'

Standing, I gave a coquettish curtsey. 'Why, Sir, I'd be delighted.' As we took to the dance floor I heard Eoghan remark to his wife, 'I think our Declan's made a friend.'

Over in the corner watching us closely stood three figures

140

leaning against the wall, pints in hand. It was the Gillivers and they weren't smiling; just watching us between puffing on cigarettes. As we danced by, I gave them a curt nod. 'Good evening boys. Got all the hawthorn spines out, I see.' With a collective sneer, they turned away.

'Bad lot those,' said Declan. 'Best not antagonise them further.'

'Why not? It's one of my particular talents.'

'And especially the big one that you skewered,' said Declan. 'Tis said they have links across the border and we don't want none of *their* kind here.' His face said he was very serious.

'Okay,' I said.

'This lovely land is troubled enough,' he said as the record ended.

Then, the whole family were up on the floor before the band came on again, each taking turns to sing at the microphone. The Irish must surely have invented karaoke years before it became popular. As the last strains of 'Jug of Punch' had been done to death, Eoghan took the microphone to loud applause from the room. I looked expectantly at Astrid. 'His party piece,' she said with the resignation of someone who had heard it hundreds of times before. Complete silence had descended on the room as he began to sing 'Danny Boy' and as he sang that beautiful song, it was all too easy to forget the troops were in Derry and the grim images of concrete walls topped with barbed wire and daubed with nationalist slogans. I shuddered as he sang. How could anyone think of spoiling this peaceful land with their bombs and guns; their hate, torment, and reprisals? Belfast and its horrors seemed a million miles away. In my mind, however, the television images of a divided, bleak-looking city like something from behind the iron curtain remained. It was where machine-gun carrying British soldiers patrolled the grey streets under constant threat of attack. It was a place of curfews, internment, and incursions over the border with the Republic, spreading fear and hate.

The songs could no longer mask the images on the news in all its dreadful glory, of shootings, maiming and bomb blasts daily, as well as the building of a new internment camp that would become the Maze. It would become infamous for the 'H' blocks and would gnaw at the collective consciousness of all free-thinking men and women for years to come.

But here, in this community, listening to Eoghan singing his plaintive song, it still felt safe. I had no way of knowing how many years it would be, that like most wars, it would take years of speculation and pain before the whole story would end – if it ever did. There would be Bloody Sunday and many more atrocities until the whole thing was dragged kicking and screaming towards the Good Friday agreement and the death throes of the 'Troubles'.

All that was impossible to imagine in a safe dance hall surrounded by green fields, a dark sky with a bright moon lying on its back amid stars and planets, and the strains of 'Danny Boy' sung at full volume in the smoky atmosphere. I listened, captivated in my own little world, mouthing the words. 'But come ye back when summer's in the meadow, or when the valley's hushed and white with snow...' And overcome by the melody, I couldn't stop myself from joining in. 'Tis I'll be here in sunshine or in shadow. Oh, Danny boy, oh, Danny boy, I love you so.'

Another voice came from behind me very close to my ear. 'Well now, that was a perfect note, so it was.'

I turned sharply, 'Sorry?'

'That last note, t'was pitch perfect.' He was standing close behind me looking down: a tall man with twinkling eyes, I found myself looking up into. They were as soft as butter. A frisson ran down my back and I caught an involuntary breath.

'It's a long time since I heard a perfect top E.' He smiled gently. 'Please tell me you *do* sing. Do *not* tell me the only time you sing is in the bath? That would be a terrible shame and a waste, so it would.'

I blustered, embarrassed, words dying in my dry throat. He had been close enough to me to hear and I'd not noticed. He reached out his hand and stroked my cheek and I was quite unable to move for a moment even though a stranger was touching me.

'Liam,' he said, above the final chorus of the song and I was unable to take my eyes away from that soft, dark complexioned face that demanded I hold his gaze. He wore a country-style, checked shirt untucked from his jeans, sleeves rolled, no, folded at the elbow. 'Will you dance with me, perhaps?' He offered his hand and raised an eyebrow that begged affirmation.

'Oh...' His eyes held me still with a magnetism I found hard to break, the pit of my stomach a tight knot and my knees had turned to jelly. He led me to the dance floor. 'My name's Paola,' I said.

He stopped and turned. 'I know that.'

I didn't ask him how.

Throughout the dance, his eyes never left my face; his hands on my shoulders were the lightest of touches. Those eyes were the colour of melted butter and caramel, and blond curls of hair meandered down to his collar. *The tawny eyes of an owl,* I thought. One could never imagine that soft, west of Ireland lilting voice being raised in anger or aggression.

The song ended, and it was time for the band to play again. Declan downed the pint of Guinness he held and headed for the stage picking up his bodhran as he went. I turned to my new friend to find him gone. I looked around a little breathlessly.

Declan's group launched into another rendition of 'Jug of Punch' to get everyone singing. Shelagh tapped me on the shoulder. 'Now we can really let our hair down and sing, Pao.'

Suddenly, I saw him, there on the stage with his guitar. It was a strange feeling. I hadn't noticed him the first time. We sang constantly for over an hour until practically hoarse until Shelagh said, 'God, I need a breath of fresh air, Pao.'

'So, do I,' I grabbed her arm and we headed for the door. Sitting on the wall outside, we kicked off our shoes. I winced. 'My feet are killing me. I haven't danced so much since...since...'

We looked at each other and said in unison, 'Since the party night in the hut.'

Shelagh gave me a sly look. 'Well, *you* seemed to be doin' pretty well for yourself in there,' she said with a backward nod to the community centre. 'A little bird is whispering in my ear that you are healing – at long last. The pain's gone from your face.' I gave her a questioning look. 'Don't deny it, Pao, you're comin' out of purdah and 'tis a wondrous sight. Don't look so worried, Pao. Yer not betraying him.'

Panic hit me like a brick. 'Robbie,' I said.

She held up a forceful finger. 'No, Pao! It's time to let him go.

Just the way you did the day he sailed away home. You did it once and now's the time to do it again, except this time it'll be harder because you have to let go for good.'

'No...' I croaked, my voice breaking.

'The only person keeping him here is you. What are you so afraid of?'

'That all we were to each other will just disappear and soon I won't even remember what he looked like or how his voice sounded...or what his touch felt like.' Emotion was taking over. 'No, I can't...not yet. I can't.'

'Isn't that because you keep going over and over it in your mind?'

'I can't stop! If I stop, I'll forget.'

Shelagh flung out her arms in a gesture of exasperation and I began to get angry. It welled up inside me like a volcano about to erupt. I had a sudden thought: 'Is that why you asked me here?' I spat. 'Because you're sick to death of me and my emotions? Of all the deceitful...conniving, cruel...'

She looked at me steadily, calmly, her lips pressed in a tight line. 'Blame me if you like, Pao. Shout at me as loud as you want if it makes you feel better. Become an old maid, hanging on to the thread of possibility for what might have been. Sorry to state the bleedin' obvious, but Robbie's dead.'

'I know he's dead!' I shrieked, my face white with temper, angry tears running down my cheeks at someone who'd had the audacity to be *that* blatant.

'And *you* are alive,' she went on calmly, 'a living, breathing, beautiful woman. And No, *that* is not the reason I asked you here. I asked you because you are my best friend and I love you and – believe it or not – I wanted you to meet my family and share them with you for a little while. Because, if you are honest with yourself, Pao, it's your memories that are hurting you; a raw spot you keep rubbing salt into. When it continues to hurt that bad you must lay him aside and move on. Learn to love again, or fade like a flower in a dry vase that no one is allowed to throw away. Clear out the mausoleum that your memory has become and let the light in.'

'I can't.' I sobbed, head bowed.

'Time is passing. Do you honestly think Robbie would have

expected you to go on grieving like this forever?' Her arms went around me, and I rested my head on her shoulder.

The truth was painful, hard, and stark to hear from my friend, Shelagh who was the only one brave enough to spell it out. Would going on grieving be any less so? Maybe it *was* time to let go of the grief – to allow myself to feel again. I wiped my nose and looked down at my little black dress. It had been raining, though neither of us had noticed, our hair hanging in wet tangles. Even if Shelagh *had* noticed, she'd been enough of a friend to have sat there anyway as mascara ran in rivulets down both our faces.

The time had come for all of us to move on.

Chapter 19

I watched Eoghan as he stood in his usual spot at the range cooking breakfast. Something was different today. His shoulders were not relaxed and he held his neck with unaccustomed rigidity. He looked troubled.

We'd seen the local TV news already. There'd been an explosion close to the border in the early hours of the morning. Two cars had been destroyed by some sort of device left under one of them, and a nearby house had been damaged. Studiously, we said nothing, though Declan made the mistake of mentioning it as he sat down at the table eliciting a sharp warning glance from his mother. It said, this was not to be discussed, either at breakfast or in front of the younger children.

Eoghan turned and shot Declan a look of caution. 'The IRA is our shame. We do not parade that shame in front of guests.'

Declan quickly got the message. 'Sorry, Da…. Paola.'

Embarrassed, I nodded and looked down at my plate. The newspapers were full of it, but I noticed they promptly disappeared after breakfast out of reach of the younger members of the family. It was the first such incident so close to home and hard to imagine. Later, I stood looking over the ocean, its surface calm, crystal and sparkling. Shelagh had gone on an errand for Astrid. 'An errand of mercy,' she'd said and not one that I would have wanted to accompany her on, so I'd planned to go down to the sea.

Aunt Philomena – aged 89 – was 'a witch and a harridan', according to Shelagh, and the reason for my being left behind was her hatred of all things British. It was nothing at all to do with the 'Troubles,' but stemmed from an unhappy love affair with an English soldier during the war. Having fallen passionately in love with this young man and pledged her life to him against the wishes of her family, he'd promptly upped and left her. Apparently, something to do with having a wife and four children in Watford! She'd neither forgiven nor forgotten, branding all Englishmen as rogues, thieves and sheep-stealers, spitting forcefully on the ground whenever that country was mentioned.

Shelagh had decided that if someone had to look in on the old lady, it better be her – and alone. So, loaded down with home-made jam, and honey from Astrid's hives, as well as Eoghan's freshly-baked bread and an apple pie, she set off down the lane accepting her fate. Waiting would be a wagging-fingered lecture on the perils of even visiting England, let alone working there.

Breathing in the sea air deeply, I paused before returning across the field and leaned on the gate. Unable to dispel the morning's events from my mind, I wondered if the 'Troubles' would spread. Surely this place could never be tainted by such things? Guns and bombs didn't belong here in the warm, wildflower meadows. Then a sudden dark thought invaded my mind. France must have been like this. The Somme was a place such as this before shells, machinery and marching feet had changed it into the stinking muddy hell it became. Suddenly, I was tired – mentally and physically. I'd had almost three years of the most demanding job and it *had* drained me – body and soul. Having to forfeit days off when we were busy, precious time lost to allow recuperation from the huge emotional strain of illness and sometimes death of those we'd lovingly cared for and got to know. There were the twelve-hour days when I'd worked overtime if there hadn't been enough staff to take over. All that was expected. The NHS survived mainly on the goodwill of its staff. It was all unpaid – for love. There *was* no additional money for overtime and it was easier to promise time off in lieu, which was rarely honoured.

I sat down on the soft grass by the gate, surrounded by buttercups and purple vetch, the scent of clover filling my nostrils and rested back on the grass. Yes, grief *was* wearisome. It was high time I stopped it. Shelagh was right; my wise counselling friend, at this moment probably getting a wigging on the dangers of collaborating with the enemy. The last year had been the longest and saddest of my life, and yet, in some ways, it had gone in the blink of an eye.

I lay on my back in the grass and gazed up at the cornflower-blue sky. There was not a cloud to be seen, the softness cradling me, as the subtle sounds of the countryside crept into my brain bringing soothing peace. Somewhere, far away, a skylark rose, singing as the hypnotic sound of the ocean rocked me gently towards sleep, as my mind drifted on a carpet of nature's softness. I dreamed of Linnie, for it was in such a meadow that I saw her a short while after she died.

I neither saw nor heard his approach. Though my eyes were closed, I suddenly became aware the sun was no longer on my face and there was a change in the light on the other side of my eyelids. I opened my eyes and looked up to see the largest of the Gilliver brothers towering over me; a look of amused menace on his face.

'Ah, pretty girl, we are alone at last, so we are. Let's see how brave yer are now.'

I struggled to a sitting position only to be shoved roughly back to the ground as he launched his body on top of me, pinning me beneath him, his offensive breath close to my face. Turning my head away in disgust, I struggled. 'Get off me, you pig,' I spat between clenched teeth.

'Oh, pig is it?' He leered at me and I felt his rough hands move down my body. 'I'd have thought with you cavortin' with pig boy, you'd be well used to the smell by now.'

Now I was really scared. His hands wandered further as I struggled to no avail beneath his weight. With one paw-like hand, he held both mine above my head, the other was already inside my thin cotton blouse. With a scream, I kicked, catching him in the kidney area with my heel, enough for him to momentarily let go of my arms, and punched him hard in the face. Blood sprayed from his nose as he exhaled with a gasp, surprised but very angry judging by the look on his face. Then, he hit me, a hard back-handed blow across the mouth that snapped my head and knocked the breath from my body. Struggling for air I was unable to scream.

He laughed – a cruel mocking sound. Time seemed to stand

still as, with his knee, he forced my legs apart. 'Now, yer filthy English proddy bitch, let's see what yer make of havin' a real man inside yer for a change. Fuckin' bitch.' He hit me again.

I froze with horror as he tore open my blouse, time still moving at a fraction of its speed in my head. *You will not let this happen. You will not die here in this field*, and with a last supreme effort I found my voice again and screamed loud enough to wake the dead, my eyes wide and staring.

There was a sudden gasp and a cry that wasn't mine and he fell sideways. I scrambled away from where he lay motionless on the ground, blood coursing from a deep wound on his head. I was still screaming. Arms were around me pulling me up, soft words were whispered in my ear. Then there was nothing but blackness.

The next time I opened my eyes, it took a few seconds to realise what had happened and I began to scream again. Pain thudded through my head and face.

'Shussh, Paola, it's okay. He can't hurt you any more now. It's over. Be still now.'

I was being carried in a firm grasp, my head resting against a soft linen shirt. Groggy and with the salty taste of blood in my mouth, I clung on allowing someone else to take charge, having little strength or fight left. Only when I opened my eyes again did I find myself looking into the soft caramel ones of Liam Hennesey and I was back at the farm.

Police sirens wailed in the distance and the smell of Padraig Gilliver had been replaced by one of freshly-washed hair.

'Don't try to talk, Paola. You'll have to speak to the Garda later...but not just yet.'

'How...?' I mumbled.

'Don't talk. It will hurt.'

It did. The left side of my face and eye felt as though they were about to explode.

'I saw him,' said Liam gently. 'I watched him follow you across the field, that Gilliver bastard and when he made his move, I ran...and only just fast enough. Thank God, my father taught me to skim stones.'

I remembered my attacker lying there, blood dripping from his head, staining the grass.

'Direct hit,' said Liam, without taking his eyes from mine.

'Liam…' I began to sob, terrified again at what almost happened there in that field, fear mixed with pain making me retch between sobs.

'You're safe now, baby.'

'Oh, Liam, I'm so…so…'

'Nothing's owed,' he whispered stroking my hair. 'Now I'm going to leave you to Astrid and Shelagh to see to that face of yours and get you all cleaned up. Courage now.'

I was having difficulty letting go of his hand.

The fury in the house was palpable, even to me in my distressed state.

'Attacked and violated, clothing torn. A guest in our country,' Eoghan raged. 'Tis a complete disgrace.' Astrid's tender touch and matter-of-fact approach was comforting. It was she who put ice on my face and held it there, despite my whimpering, and kept everything calm and normal, as though attempted rape and assault was something she was called on to deal with every day. I was grateful for that. It was *she* who sat beside me holding my hand when the Garda came – uniformed men and women to take statements and ask interminable questions. They assured me that Padraig Gilliver was in custody and that I was safe. The whole process was an ordeal but made much easier by the presence of my adopted Irish step-mama.

'Astrid, thank you,' I whispered, after the police had left. I took her hand again. 'I want to put it behind me now. I don't want anyone to treat me differently or be walking on eggshells around me.'

She smiled and patted my hand. 'What…in *this* house? Ach, we get on with things here.' I nodded to her in appreciation as she went to the kitchen to make coffee.

I looked in the mirror. My face was a mess. An angry, red bruise had formed under my swollen eye and a long, red wheal ran down my cheek to a split lip. 'Wonderful,' I said to my reflection, tentatively touching the swelling and wincing, 'bloody wonderful! Now, put *that* painful memory in the past where it belongs – in a sealed box where you never need look at it again.' Realistically, I knew whenever I caught my reflection – for a while at least – I'd be back in that field. Getting over an experience like that is never so simple. But since my chat with Shelagh I'd made myself a promise that memories would never be allowed to hurt me again. So, nodding assent to my reflection, I went down to supper, every tooth feeling as if it had been knocked out and put back in again.

From outside the kitchen door I could hear the twins squabbling loudly. 'But it's not right, is it? What do you think, Siobhan?'

'Jesus will punish him, Cass. Papa says Jesus will always punish sinners and so will our Lady. She will, but to make sure I made the daisy ring and put it under me pillow.'

'Oh, Siobhan, you never.'

'Like the fairies told us to do if it was something *really* bad and I don't care. You should make one too, Cass, just to be sure. Then we must speak the words together.'

'The words the fairies taught us?'

'Yes, Cass, and *I'll* be doin' the talking.'

'And why should it be you?'

'Because,' came the petulant reply, 'I'm the oldest and so that makes me the best at it.'

'That's not fair,' whined Cass. 'I'm going to tell the fairies that you *never* let me say the words.'

'You go then...I bet you're a scaredy-cat to go without your big sister to keep you safe.'

'You're *not* bigger!' There was the unmistakable sound of a foot stamp.

'But I'm older.'

'Only five minutes.'

'There you are then.' Another louder stamp.

'*You* can spit on the daisies,' said Siobhan by way of acquiescence.

'*I'm* goin' to ask the fairies to send a bolt of lightning to get the nasty man and he'll burn in hell and cry for his mammy, so he will, and she won't come because the little people won't let her.'

It was clearly time to intervene, so I made a deliberate noise and immediately heard loud 'shushing'. Two little angels, with corn-coloured curls that danced with each movement, quickly pulled out chairs to sit at the kitchen table as the rest of the family began to assemble for supper.

Astrid appeared and began to serve dinner. Without comment she gave me the softest-to-chew option. Silently I blessed her knowing that eating for the next few days was not going to be easy or hold its usual pleasures.

What did I make of the twins? I found myself wondering as we ate, squabbling like fury one minute, and plotting retribution and revenge the next. They still believed in the divine. How wonderful to be able to rely on the certainty to punish transgressors and not on the law of the land. For a moment I wished I had their faith. In a day or two I'd have to stand before a magistrate and re-live the whole thing. I wasn't looking forward to it. I was still an outsider and could hear, 'filthy, English, proddy bitch' ringing in my ears. Those hateful words made my legs turn to jelly.

And, I'd have to face *him* – Padraig Gilliver – across a courtroom and would feel his hatred assaulting me again.

The family was incredible. Not once did the incident enter conversation, which was the best thing that could have happened. For it wouldn't have allowed the wound in my memory to heal and I reasoned that if I could keep it all together, then in a few short days it would all be over. I had another ten glorious days here to belong and be cherished and to walk the lanes and fields without fear – or so I thought.

Chapter 20

'Paola...Paola,' Eoghan's melodious voice drifted down the garden path to where Shelagh and I were sitting alongside the pond watching the dragon flies dance their aerial ballet above us. I waved as he approached. 'Well now, Paola, you have a visitor – a dashingly handsome prince to sweep you off your feet, no doubt.

'Da, have you been reading too many of Ma's Mills and Boon?' said Shelagh with an amused raise of her eyebrows.

I laughed and quickly winced. Although some of the swelling had gone down, there was still a large multi-coloured bruise across my cheek and mouth.

'Ach, there's not enough romance in the world any more,' he replied sagely, shaking his head. 'Now in my day...'

'Da,' interrupted Shelagh, 'who is it?'

'It's a young fella with a picnic basket,' he said, 'and if I'm not very much mistaken judgin' by the smell of aftershave he seems to have bathed in, he's come a-courtin'.

I smiled, carefully, 'Oh, Eoghan, really now.'

He raised his arm and indicated behind him. Liam walked slowly down the path towards us, a large wicker basket in one hand, his guitar slung loosely across his back.

He smiled broadly. 'My, you're looking a treat now, Paola.'

'No, I'm not. I look as though I lost a fight with a boxing kangaroo.'

'Rubbish,' retorted Eoghan. 'Now, don't be keeping the poor boy waiting. Get away and have your picnic on the beach on this lovely day.' He turned. 'Shelagh, I need your help.'

She scowled. 'Doing what?'

'I'll think of something.' He grinned.

I turned, concerned. Oh, Shelagh, if you *do* mind, I won't go.

After all we can always sit here in the...'

'Oh, get on with yer,' she said, with a wave of her hand, muttering. 'I wish someone would take *me* for a beach picnic and...'

'No, Shelagh, I'm sure Liam wouldn't mind if we...'

'Not on yer life,' she said, holding up both hands in submission, taking Eoghan's enormous hint, 'children to feed, dogs to wash...thumbs to twiddle.'

I gave her a reproachful look, but her expression was one of determination. 'For heaven's sake go.' Her bottom lip quivered with ill-disguised mirth. 'And have fun.' She winked over her shoulder as Eoghan hurried her back up the path.

Liam shook his head as we watched them go. 'Paola, I have known that woman all me life and she's about as subtle as a pork pie at a Jewish weddin,' so she is. I hope you don't think...you aren't.... Ach, I'm babbling. Shall we do as she says and just go?'

I spun on my heels. 'Come on, Liam, race you to the beach.' I set off running.

'Hey, just a minute,' he cried. 'I got stuff to carry.'

'Then, it'll be a fair race.' I called over my shoulder as I ran. I glanced back. He was gaining on me despite his guitar and large basket. I jumped over the style into the hay meadow and froze. Carried away with the moment, I hadn't given it a thought. I stared. A little way ahead and offset from the path was the flattened grass that marked the site of my struggle with the unwelcome attentions of Padraig Gilliver. Horror seized the pit of my stomach and I sank to the ground. 'Filthy, fuckin, proddy bitch!' Unable to tear my eyes away from the spot, a scream died, in my throat.

'Paola!' Liam had caught up and dropping his burden, cupped a hand over both my shoulders. 'It's okay...he can't hurt you now.' He held me until my heart stopped its frantic pounding and I could finally breathe again. 'Tis just a place, Paola. The land swallows up badness and memory and next spring there'll be no trace. Let it go. This does not belong here in the sweet thoughts of a lovely woman. Hold my hand, now.'

And without another backward glance, we walked across the field. My legs were once again steady, taking strength from Liam's firm grip on my hand.

We spread out the picnic rug that had been stowed in the lid of the basket on the soft sand, a little way back from the water-line with its detritus of shells and seaweed left by the retreating tide. The grasses that held the dunes stable, waved, caught by puffs of breeze, welcome on such a hot afternoon.

Liam certainly knew how to pack a picnic basket. Rather cynically, I wondered how often he'd done this. *Why do you think like that?* I remonstrated with myself. Of course, I knew very well. It was Robbie who had dating women down to a fine art and a method he'd repeated time after time, honing his craft to perfection with every new conquest. I checked myself. This was not Robbie. It was Liam. Did I believe that all men were alike or had I the right to invent a history I'd no way of knowing? The fact was I didn't really care – not at that moment. This man had saved me from further degradation and injury. He may have even saved my life, but it wasn't gratitude that had brought me to this beach with him. It was something entirely different – a genuine attraction and the prospect of spending a pleasant afternoon with a good-looking and interesting man who seemed to like my company too.

'How long has the band been going?' I asked, nibbling on another ham roll, hoping it didn't come from one of Declan's pigs, as by now, I knew them all by name.

'Jimmy Leary and I knew each other at junior school since we were nippers and we played in the school band. Moz and Dec joined later, but we only do it for pleasure – local stuff mostly.'

'You're good.'

He touched his forelock in a self-deprecating gesture. 'Why, thank you, my dear. Dec plays a pretty mean bodhran, doesn't he?'

'I've never heard anything like it,' I said.

'You see, we Irish are born with the music in us. We get it from the tit, so to speak. Sorry, from our mother's milk.'

I chanced a laugh. It still hurt.

'But you sing,' he went on, 'and don't say you do not because I heard you. You have near-perfect pitch.'

'I hadn't sung for ages,' I said, 'not until the other night.

'Well now, that's a cryin' shame, so it is.' He didn't ask why, and I was grateful, just wanting to enjoy the afternoon for what it was. After the picnic was finished, we drank lemonade, lay on the blanket in the sunshine and talked...and talked.

His father was a builder, running his own business just outside Sligo town and his mother was sister-in-charge of the local casualty department in the nearby general hospital. 'So, we lads – that's father, brother James and me, well, we're all pretty handy at taking care of ourselves. I taught meself to cook for our survival a long time ago.' He looked at my dubious expression. 'Now don't look so surprised; it's not just the beans on toast. I can do posh stuff too.'

'Not just a pretty face then, 'I teased.

'I can turn me hand to most things – apart from the paid day job.'

'And that is?'

'Guess.'

'I've not the faintest idea.'

'Go on, take a guess,' he insisted.

'I have no idea. God...I dunno. Car mechanic? Tailor's dummy? I know: ballet dancer, and a part-time male model.'

'Get away woman.' He threw back his head and laughed.

'Thief, then,' I said, 'Braggard, knight in shining armour rescuing maidens in distress.' I became serious. 'Well, you certainly did that for me and I want you to know I *am* grateful, Liam.'

'I don't want or need you to be grateful, Paola. I want...'

I looked up quickly. 'Yes?'

He hesitated. 'I want you to listen.' He reached for his guitar. The strong light of the afternoon was softening though neither of us had noticed. Liam dusted a few grains of sand from the face of the guitar and began to play. 'I wrote you a song, Paola.'

'You did? Why?'

'Because deep down I'm a shy Irish fella who finds it hard to say things sometimes.' He began to sing, 'Would you dance, if I asked you in the soft, evening light, pressed close to my body, would you save my soul tonight?' The words were evocative. I never took my eyes from his face as he sang, and I sat mesmerised until he was finished. 'That's beautiful,' I said. 'How long did it take to write that?'

'Oh, not long, when I realised who I was writing it for.' His eyes held mine much longer than it took to reply. He put his guitar aside and I rested my head in his lap allowing the sound of the waves to do the talking. Carefully, he traced my eyebrows with his finger and gently down my nose, then leaning forward, kissed the tip lightly with a touch as soft as a butterfly.

A quiver of pleasure spread to the pit of my stomach and down to my toes. It didn't feel odd or unwelcome, because at that moment I wanted him like I'd never wanted anyone for a long time, with a need that set my soul screaming for his body, his touch. He got to his feet and taking my hand, pulled me to mine. Then his arms encircled my body, his mouth finding my own, gently. Despite my injuries, my whole body responded to his kiss, deeper and deeper, until he swept me into his arms. This time, as he carried me, my head against his soft shirt, I was neither hurt nor afraid.'

He touched my lip. 'Does it hurt?'

'Yes.'

The rocks and soft sand between provided a soft, private bed as we made love to each other with only breaking waves and the cries of the seabirds mingling with those of our own.

'Liam, I don't want you to think...'

He placed a finger to my lips. 'I don't think anything, Paola, only that I'm probably falling in love with you and I wanted to show you. Did I do that, or are you mortally offended by such a forward gesture from someone you barely know?'

'None of those things,' I whispered, our eyes still holding, until once more our bodies melted together in a deep, satisfying climactic impact. Still shuddering from our lovemaking, Liam's hand caressed my cheek and gazing into those caramel eyes, I knew I was mended. I'd come to Ireland still a broken soul and now that soul was healed. As we held each other, I knew now I *could* move on.

The tide was rising fast with the fading light, as we dusted sand from our clothing and walked hand in hand back to the farmhouse.

As we rounded the corner at the bottom of the path that led to the house, we saw them; two Garda vehicles parked side by side.

'Oh, no...' I began.

'Tis okay, Paola. They usually visit before a court appearance to let you know what's expected. It will just be to give you a bit of support, that's all. Nothin' to be worryin' yerself about.'

Astrid and Shelagh had come out to meet us, their faces betraying nothing.

'Paola,' said Astrid, 'the police are here to see you. Something serious has happened I'm afraid.' Liam and I exchanged worried glances and I quickened my step. 'They're in the front parlour,' said Astrid. 'Liam,' I heard her say, 'stay awhile – you'll be needed, I fancy.'

The officers stood as I entered, both holding large mugs of coffee, judging by the smell. One was a woman in a peaked cap. She walked over to me and smiled, indicating the sofa. 'Come and sit, Miss Green.' I did, and she sat beside me while the male stood opposite. Both removed their hats, the woman officer patting her hair.

'What's happened?' I began, 'is it bad news from England?'

The male officer held up a hand. 'No, Miss, nothing like that. This morning there was an explosion at the police station in Newry; most probably a bomb. Two policemen and a prisoner were killed. We're here to tell you that the prisoner in question was Padraig Gilliver.'

My hands went up to my face in shock. Unable to speak, my thoughts raced, and my head began to spin wildly. He was dead – *that* man. There was a huge mixture of emotions and I felt the colour drain from my face. Suddenly, I had an overwhelming sense of guilt that no matter what had occurred, three men were dead because of me. I must have swayed a little, because Eoghan, who had been standing with his back to the window, hands deep in his pockets, rushed forward to pour a glass of water. Holding my trembling hands, he steadied the glass while I drank.

'I'm afraid we must go over a few things again, Miss Green, in the light of events and ask you some more questions, because this changes things somewhat.' The male officer spoke quietly but firmly.

'For a start, you won't have to go through the ordeal of going to court now, Paola,' said Eoghan. 'And–'

'But there *are* other matters,' interrupted the woman officer. 'Are you ready to answer some more questions now?'

My mind was still whirling. *Three men are dead because of me.* The phrase repeated over and over.

'Miss Green...'

'Yes, I think so, Officer.'

She continued. 'We need to go through the alleged attack on you, Miss Green.'

'Alleged?' I fingered my painful cheek and the bruised area below my eye.

'I'm sorry, but even though Gilliver was formally charged we still have to refer to it as such.'

'Yes, of course. I suppose so.'

The male officer continued. 'Shortly before the blast, Gilliver complained of dizziness and pain in his head. The duty police doctor was called to examine him but was unable to attend before the explosion. So, at this time, we don't know if he was suffering from a head injury that led to his death or whether he died as a result of the explosion. We know he had some degree of injury to his head from a stone thrown by...' he took out his notebook and referred to it 'by Liam Hennesey.'

'Yes, but...' Alarm bells began to ring in my head – and I didn't like where this was leading. 'Sir, had Mr. Hennesey not acted in the way he did, I'd have certainly been raped or worse. That's what Gilliver said he was going to do to me.'

'Okay, that's fine. Nevertheless, a man is dead. I believe you were in the company of Liam Hennesey today. When today exactly?'

'All afternoon – until just now.'

'Where did you go?'

'To the beach.' I shifted uncomfortably under his steady gaze.

'For what purpose?'

'We had a picnic.'

He wrote in his notebook. 'What time did he come to collect you? He *did* come here to collect you I take it?'

I looked at Eoghan.

'Must have been about one, or perhaps one-thirty?' I said.

He nodded.

'If you don't mind me saying so, Miss Green, it was a *very* long picnic.'

'We talked a lot,' I said rather lamely, blushing furiously.

Eoghan got to his feet and addressed the officer. 'Now, now, Phelan, don't be badgering the girl. Were you never young yourself? Can you not remember canoodlin' with a girl in your arms and how the hours just slipped away? Shame on you!'

I was now bright red in the face and unable to look at Eoghan, for I felt he knew *exactly* what we'd been doing.

The officer turned his attention back to me. 'So, Mr. Henessey saved you? And now you're his girlfriend. Is that right?'

'No...yes...no,' I spluttered. 'I mean that I don't know him very well. We only recently met, but I *do* like him.'

'A lot?'

'Yes, I suppose so.'

'And he likes you? A lot?'

'I think so.' I began to shuffle uncomfortably again.

'So,' he went on, thoughtfully, 'it would be very natural then, that, having defended you once, he'd want to make *absolutely* sure that Padraig Gilliver couldn't hurt you again?'

I was horror-struck at what he seemed to be suggesting. 'What are you saying?' I demanded.

'That Mr. Henessey had the time to go to Newry and make *very* sure that Gilliver *couldn't* hurt you again?'

'No!' I protested. 'Liam wouldn't hurt a fly. He's gentle and kind and...'

'How do you know, Miss Green? You say you only just met him. So, how do you know?'

'I...I...'

Liam had been sitting on the wall outside talking to Astrid when the two came out to take him away for questioning. With firm hands on his shoulders they led him towards the police car. He did not resist.

'No!' I shouted as they put him in the back of the car. 'Liam, Liam.... No!'

'Paola, it's all right,' he shouted through the open door. 'This will be cleared up soon. 'Tis okay.'

I clung to Eoghan, sobbing. 'No, Papa,' I whimpered. 'What is it with me? I must be cursed or something because people keep dying around me. There was a friend – two in fact – and now this. I seem to attract bad things. I come to this beautiful country and am welcomed into your family and what happens? I bring chaos…and death…and shame to you all. I must go home before anything else bad happens.'

Eoghan held me at arms' length, a gentle yet stern look in his eyes. 'Now, you look here, young woman,' he began, 'don't you dare be blamin' yerself. As you say, this country is indeed beautiful, but it's still sullied by evil men in the name of progress and freedom. The IRA is the ones causing chaos, not you. So, I never want to hear you say that again.' His grip remained firm on my shoulders. 'And, I'll wager it was *them* behind that bomb. They'd have been after the kudos of killing a few Garda. As for Gilliver, he was just in the wrong place at the wrong time. Or maybe it was natural justice, because I happen to know that family have links with the boyos over the border. So, they've probably just taken out one of their own without knowin' it. I'll bet you that come the funeral, the family will be followed by a bunch of figures, black-clad and wearing masks, shooting off their weapons over the grave as they bury the bastard.'

Eoghan's unaccustomed candour made me gasp.

'Sorry, Paola. We are living in a very dangerous part of the world. And, it's us who should be apologising to you. You came here as a guest of our daughter and look what's happened. It's us who failed to keep you safe from the Gillivers.'

'I don't think the episode at the pigsty helped,' I said. 'I antagonised him.'

'No, Paola, they'd just be looking for an excuse – a soft target. Well,' his lips twitched a little, 'certainly got *that* wrong, didn't they? A dab hand with a pitchfork, so I hear.' He took a deep breath. 'Now, we are going to forget it, and don't you go bothering yerself with any guilty thoughts again.' He let go of my shoulders. 'You *are* very safe here. All my boys and girls would defend you to the last and my wife is a crack shot with her pigeon gun in the vegetable patch.'

Tears welled in my eyes again. 'Oh, Eoghan…' I began.

'And don't go worryin' about Liam. He's innocent, you'll see.'

Next day, Liam was formally cleared of any wrong-doing. He was released, and after seeing his family, the next thing he did was come to the farm to find me. I ran to meet him and held him longer than would have been usual when greeting a mere friend.

'See, Paola,' he whispered in my ear, his face close to my cheek, 'no evidence and the post-mortem will prove it.'

'When?'

'Tomorrow. The police here don't hang about these days. The boyos satisfaction at taking out two officers will be dampened by accidentally killing one of their own.'

'So, he was IRA?'

'It was always suspected.'

'I'm pleased you're home, Liam,' I whispered.

'Me mammy was glad to see me.'

'So am I.'

'I was rather hoping you might be. Now, let's put it behind us.' He kissed my forehead gently as Eoghan came forward to shake his hand.

The post-mortem showed that Gilliver had been blown to pieces. There was no evidence and no case to answer. A few days later, as Eoghan had predicted, there *were* men in black at his funeral, firing a volley of shots into the sky over the grave as the Gilliver family looked on. I'd watched the TV from the back of the room near the door as the local news covered it some days later, unable to sit or even stand near to the images. It was over, and during the next ten days, I slowly came to believe it.

Whatever was happening in the north, peace had returned to this corner of Ireland. Terrible things were undoubtedly still happening, but it was not to impact on us again. There was perhaps a distant – very distant – branch of the family that sympathised with the struggles in the north, but *this* part of it was well-removed from that. I never heard Shelagh refer to it again – drunk or sober.

For the rest of my stay in Ireland, the sun shone and all of us continued to eat, drink, and laugh together. The twins remained friends with the fairies and elves. Declan tended his beloved pigs and practised the bodhran long into the night in the hay barn well away from the house, at Astrid's insistence. She continued to tend her garden and the bees; Eoghan, his cooking range and pots, still polishing them after every meal. Shelagh and I walked for miles in the countryside and visited the Ballygawley Mountains, picnicking in woodland and by the lakes.

And there was *still* a little time when no one chose to notice my absence to meet Liam on the beach by the rocks to talk, laugh and make love as if we'd known each other for a lifetime.

All too soon, it was time to say our goodbyes and make promises to 'come back soon'. With a large bag of Astrid's cakes shoved in our rucksacks, we boarded the local taxi. There were tears in my eyes and a very large lump in my throat.

'Don't you dare cry,' ordered Shelagh out of the corner of her mouth without looking at me.

My eyes held Liam's as the taxi began to pull away from the sea of waving hands, shouts from the children running alongside and blown kisses.

'I love you, Paola,' he shouted at the top of his voice without a care for who was listening – and Shelagh gave me her enigmatic, Mona Lisa smile.

Chapter 21

'Oh no, not male medics again!' I exclaimed as I read the list that had been posted on the dining room wall. 'Welcome home, Paola.' I felt I'd done my share in the galley of *that* particular slave ship.

It was September and only two weeks to our final exams. I should have been quaking in my diminutive boots as most members of our year were – but I wasn't. Could it have been the warm feeling in the pit of my stomach whenever I thought of Sligo? Each day brought a wave of pleasure that made everything new and worthwhile somehow, full of hope and promise again. It was absolutely nothing to do with the prospect of finally qualifying as a nurse; much more to do with twinkling eyes, breeze-ruffled hair and the soft caress of a gentle lover.

Today though, after a late-night pouring over textbook after textbook, I was in a less than affable mood. That, and the prospect of the male medical ward with its heavy lifting and coronary care unit, was not one I was relishing as I walked out of the nurses' home in the early morning. There was a chill in the air. Autumn would soon turn to winter. In a few short weeks *and* with a huge slice of luck, I'd be crossing this car park dressed rather differently in the purple uniform of a newly-qualified staff nurse. I remembered what Tissie had intoned on more than one occasion. 'Then you can *really* begin to learn, my dears.'

It's a funny thing about holidays. Once back in your familiar environment it takes all of ten minutes for you to feel like you've never been away.

We sat in Sister's office, notebooks in hand, poised and ready for the night staff to give the handover so they could escape to their beds. It was a grim picture. Coronary Care was full – probably due to the approach of winter when people take less exercise and more food. Whatever the reason, it was still full of elderly men hooked up to heart monitors. I quite liked working with coronary patients. The unpredictability of recovery in those days added excitement in a strange sort of way – for me if not the patients. Nowadays, the identification of the 'golden hour' during which treatment with Aspirin is essential has improved outcomes enormously.

But it wasn't my fate to be allocated there today. Soon everyone had been given a workload – except me. I was about to raise my hand in a gesture that said 'Hello…I'm still here. What about me?' By now, I was convinced a telling-off was coming as everyone else moved off to get on with the day's chores. After three weeks away I hadn't had time to do anything wrong surely?

Sister turned. 'Sorry, Nurse Green. I've not forgotten you.' She rose and closed the door and sat at her desk again. 'I don't know if you've heard on the grapevine, but one of our senior consultants is a patient on this ward. He's in Room 8 – the single room.'

'No, Sister. I haven't.'

'Unfortunately, he has an aggressive form of bowel cancer. His surgery was ten days ago, and he's recovered well from that, though the tumour was very advanced. He's had a complete rectal resection and has a colostomy. Intravenous fluids are in progress and he may have as much Morphine as he needs. I do *not* want to go in there and find he's in distress, Nurse Green. Do you understand me?' She was threateningly serious though I saw there was also deep compassion in her eyes. 'He must have two-hourly changes of position and *meticulous* attention to pressure areas – and spotlessly clean bedding at all times. You'll be responsible for his care.'

'Yes, Sister,' I said as she paused for breath.

'Any questions?'

I look puzzled. 'Yes, Sister. It's just that…that…'

'Spit it out, girl.'

'Well, is it appropriate, Sister?'

'Is what appropriate?'

'That I look after a senior consultant, Sister? I'm only a student nurse after all.'

'The patient made a special request that you were to care for him, Nurse.'

I stared, wondering how that was possible. 'Yes, Sister?'

She stood and folded her arms. 'Aren't you going to ask the patient's name?'

'Sorry, Sister. Of course.'

'It's Sir Ivor and you will *not* discuss his care with anyone except me. And be sure to give him anything he wants.'

It felt like I'd been hit with a brick as I drifted aimlessly down the long ward corridor, a hundred worries and questions in my head. And at the top of the list was, 'Bloody hell. Why me?' I reached the room and tapped on the door. Receiving no reply, I opened it quietly.

I was shocked.

I know I'd not seen him for a couple of months, but now the big, boisterous man I'd challenged on so many occasions, be it regarding white coats or hot water bottles, was now a shadow of his former self. He lay in the bed propped up on snowy-white pillows; his pale complexion not too far from blending in completely. His features now bore little resemblance to those that had bellowed at me. He'd lost a lot of weight, his cheekbones standing out and the skin pinched around them. I drew in a sharp breath, sorry to see the deterioration in such a short time. A change in his breathing pattern signalled waking. I stood at the foot of the bed, hands resting on the rail. He stirred, slowly opened his eyes and sighed deeply while trying to focus.

'Hello Sir Ivor,' I said quietly, not liking the fact that the boot was on the other foot. The power base had shifted, and it didn't seem right. I felt an overwhelming sense of pity.

He raised his hand and wagged a finger at me. 'Don't you dare!'

'What's that, Sir Ivor?'

'Don't think I can't see it in those lap-dog eyes of yours. Don't you dare pity me, young woman.'

'I wouldn't dream of it, Sir,' I lied unconvincingly.

'I don't want you to go thinking that you can take advantage of the situation, because woe-betide you when I'm back on my feet.'

He won't be, said a voice behind my left ear.

'Sir, I wouldn't dare exploit any situation. Like you say, when you're back on your feet...'

He won't be, repeated the voice.

Sir Ivor gave me a reproachful look and raised his eyebrows. 'Don't worry, Nurse, I won't be – you already know that.'

'Please don't be silly, Sir,' I said. 'That's rubbish.'

'Nurse Green, I would *really* appreciate it if we could stop pussyfooting around each other. I will die soon. I know it and so do you. So, if we *could* cease from wasting any more of my precious time by lying to each other, I'd be grateful. Let me explain.'

'One moment, Sir. I thought you couldn't stand the sight of me particularly after...'

'My knife-throwing act,' he said. 'And there was your outburst – quite unwarranted given the circumstances I thought but it keeps them on their toes.'

I opened my mouth to speak in defence of the poor theatre orderly he'd almost skewered to the wall but before I was able to utter a word he carried on.

'It's all right, Nurse. Truce. I was wrong. May peace reign between the two of us?'

Was that an apology? Good God!

'I asked for you because I don't want some namby-pamby, kiss-my-arse nursing sister with wrinkles and whiskers on her chin fawning over me. Neither do I want any hand-on-heart, vestal virgin of a matron who smells of mothballs looking after me either. What I want is someone with fighting spirit who won't feel sorry for me or intimidated by this irascible old sod. Someone who will make me do what's right even when I insist I know best. In short, Paola Green, you!'

I became aware that my mouth was wide open. I closed it, swallowing hard.

'Oh, sit down on the bed, for Christ's sake, Paola. It's okay. Sister won't come in without knocking – the insufferable woman bloody-well daren't. I chucked my slippers at her last time she came in and she was lucky I didn't have anything heavier to hand.' He patted the quilt and I sat. 'Now let's establish a few ground rules.'

'Ground rules?' I asked.

170

'From now on, I'm not Sir Ivor and not Sir. I'm Ivor, plain and simple, and I'd be really pleased if you call me that – in here anyway. I will call you Paola, if you'll permit me.'

'Certainly. Are you in pain?'

He wrinkled his nose and shuffled in the bed. 'Yes, since you ask.'

'Then I'll get you your Morphine and how about a cup of tea?'

'That would be lovely.'

I decided to dip my toe in the water. 'Or perhaps a hot water bottle?'

He scowled then laughed. 'Don't push your luck, child.'

I smirked. His hatred of hot water bottles was legendary. The first thing the nurses in Casualty did was frisk the blankets for the offending items before Sir Ivor arrived. If he found one that had evaded the search, it rapidly became airborne and for whoever happened to be in the line of trajectory it was tough luck! No one knew the origin of this idiosyncrasy and no one had ever been brave enough to ask.

I returned with his pain relief medication and a staff nurse to check and countersign the prescription chart. I noted he was written up for as much Morphine as required to get on top of the pain. There was a small 't' in the lower left corner of the chart. It stood for 'terminal'.

Staff Nurse Olsen grimaced as we approached the room. 'You must have upset someone pretty badly to get this job, Nurse Green?'

'No problem,' I said, 'he's a pussycat really.'

'Does insanity run in your family?' She gave me a look somewhere between disbelief and pity. We checked Ivor's wristband against the chart and with a quick 'Can you manage?' she was gone.

'Now, which bit of you has the most flesh on it, young man?' I enquired lightly.

'Oh,' he said under this breath, 'now everyone's a comedian. Why don't you try my hairy arse, Paola?'

I helped him turn onto his side and parted his gown. 'Sorry about this,' I said noticing his hip bones were getting a bit red from sitting. Quickly and without further ceremony I administered the injection. 'Sorry to have to do these personal things for

171

you, Si…Ivor but while you're on your side, I'm just going to treat those pressure areas.' I set about the job of washing, massaging, creaming and then padding out the bonier bits. Finally, I changed the sheets and re-arranged his pillows, so he was able to drink from a proper cup and not the feeder with a spout that had been left full of tea on the locker.

With care, comes pride and part of that care is to make sure the patient retains his. Somewhere between the two, comes love. I wasn't sure where the thought came from, but it came nevertheless. I smiled knowing that someone was always there to remind me why I was doing this each day. I could have chosen an easier path in life surely but where would have been the satisfaction in that?

After I'd made him comfortable he touched my hand. 'Thank you, Paola.'

'You're very welcome, Ivor. Are you tired?' It was obvious that even a little effort made him weary. It was hard to believe his condition had deteriorated so rapidly.

'Morphine and effort, I expect,' he said.

'Then I'll leave you to sleep.' I placed the call button alongside his hand. 'Ring if you need me.' His eyes closed, and I left quietly.

'Nurse Green, I'm impressed,' said Sister Jones. 'He doesn't appear to have eaten you alive. He threw his blooming slippers at me!'

He was still asleep when I went off duty. I left a little note on his locker to say I'd see him in the morning. I carried a feeling of heaviness that was nothing to do with the workload. The hold we have on life is tenuous at best. How can we know when all we have will suddenly disappear? That night I was a troubled soul. Sleep didn't come easily.

'Did you have a reasonable night, Ivor?' Morning had come all too quickly.

'They kept me well under so from a pain point of view, yes. But that big, fat, staff nurse…' I winced, 'threw me around like a sack of King Edwards. She is *very* heavy-handed, Paola. I'm extremely glad to see you.'

I washed and settled him sitting up in bed, so he could eat breakfast properly – the little he had – a bit of toast. But I'd made sure it was fresh and soft and not like the rubbery stuff that had been in the warming trolley. At one point his hand began to shake and our eyes met. 'This is a bugger, Paola – a fine mess this is!'

I helped him cut the toast into manageable pieces. 'Are you afraid, Ivor?' I asked presently.

He finished chewing the last piece. 'Tell me why I shouldn't be.'

'Because,' I began, watching him closely, 'death is a part of life and it's just another leg of the journey, surely?'

'What a perceptive young woman you are, Paola Green.' He washed down the last piece of toast with his drink. 'Did you know that when we die we come back as animals? What animal do you suppose I'll come back as?'

'A bear,' I said without hesitation, remembering how he used to look, lumbering about his world beyond the blue swing doors, growling at everyone and doing things his way. I looked at him now. 'Definitely a bear – a grumpy old bear,' I laughed. His body may have changed but the spirit in his eyes was still there in all its glory.

He laughed. 'I think it's almost time I went into hibernation for a long, long winter sleep, don't you?'

'No,' I said firmly. 'It's not winter just yet. There's still some warmth in the sun.'

With our eyes locked together we understood each other perfectly.

'So, what about me?' I asked. 'What would I come back as?'

He thought for a moment. 'Now, let me see…something small and annoying. I know, a mosquito, buzzing around the place annoying the hell out of everyone.'

'What, me?' How can you say that?' I was laughing now.

'Fragile thing with a nasty nip, but one that leaves an impression I think, Paola. You see, years ago I lived and worked with the Eskimos, or to give them their proper title, the Inuit. I was with them for seven years and those years were the happiest of my life. *They* believe we return as animals. Alaska's cold, with ice and snow so deep you'd think all civilized life would stop, but it doesn't. Everyone's used to it you see and the cold's balanced by the warmth of those wonderful people – helped by a few thick layers of caribou fur.' He yawned wearily but still talked about his country, his people and their beliefs for a little longer until his voice began to weaken with the effort. 'Will you do something for me, Paola?'

'Of course. If I can.'

'Will you read to me? There's a book of sonnets in the locker there.'

'I opened the locker and found a beautifully bound, tooled-leather book. 'I hope I can do them justice,' I said.

He closed his eyes. 'You will.'

I sat back in the chair by the bed, opened the book and began to read from Shakespeare.

'Shall I compare thee to a summer's day? Thou art more lovely, and more temperate: rough winds do shake the darling buds of May...'

Presently, he was sleeping, and I gently closed the book, placing it on top of the bedside locker.

I read many sonnets in the coming days as slowly and peacefully Ivor began to slip away. Silent, as his life ebbed and flowed towards its conclusion. Sometimes, I just sat and watched, lost in my own thoughts. He was a brilliant, though completely irascible tyrant of a man at times, with no one to be with him at the end. Maybe there hadn't been *room* for family in his life. Is that the price paid for a career such as his? How little we really know people. It made me sad though I dared not show it for he certainly would have known. It was just a week before my finals and my mind was not where it should have been. But I didn't care.

On the last day of his life he was lucid, comfortable and clearly wished to talk. 'I'm going back to Alaska, Paola, home to my Inuit family. I've left provision in my will and precise instructions.' Reaching out, he shakily took both my hands in his. 'It's been a joy to know you, Paola Green.' It was obvious that speaking was an effort. 'When you came into my kingdom through those blue doors...I knew we'd call a truce...one day. You'll make a wonderful nurse.'

'Do you think so?' There were tears in my eyes.

He brushed away one that escaped down my cheek. 'And...tell

174

him...he's a very lucky man...whoever he is...be it doctor...beggar...thief?' He was having difficulty breathing now and I propped him up on another soft pillow. 'Kingdoms are won...and lost, Paola...so are battles...and mine is nearly over.'

I stroked his hand. 'No.'

'Yes,' his voice gained strength again. 'Now go and make a cup of tea.' He gently squeezed my hand. 'I won't go whilst you're here.'

'Sorry, I'm staying anyway, Ivor.'

'Bugger off...and get me...a...coffee then.'

And when I returned, he'd closed his eyes for the last time. His kingdom beyond the blue swing doors was no more.

Chapter 22

'Why the devil we have to wear uniform to sit a three-hour exam, He only knows!' grumbled Shelagh.

I turned to her. 'Who? The Devil?'

'At the moment, Pao, I wouldn't care if I had to sell me soul to Old Nick himself so long as he comes up with the answers to the damned anatomy questions. Oh, I'd feel much better in me jumper and jeans, so I would.'

'Perhaps you'd like your comfy slippers too?' I said out of the corner of my mouth.

'There will be *no* talking now, Nurses,' barked the command. 'It's exam rules from here on so it's *no* communication *whatsoever*.' The last word was verbally underlined in bold type from Matron's lips. She was on hand to make sure we showed up and were properly turned out, no doubt hoping to witness our final humiliation. The class of '67 all looked petrified. 'All right, Nurses. You may turn over your papers and begin. You have three hours.' That short period would decide our futures.

Three hours and a great deal of writer's cramp later, I laid down my pen.

'To the Shakespeare pub,' commanded Shelagh, 'uniform or no bloody uniform.'

For the first half hour we drank in silence until, after three large gin and tonics, Shelagh began to laugh – at first a mere titter, progressing to a full-throated guffaw with tears rolling unimpeded down her pink cheeks.

'Are you okay?' I ventured with caution worried that her wee Irish lid had finally flipped.

She looked up from between near-hysterical outbursts of mad laughter. 'Don't you see, Pao? 'Tis over. Tis feckin' over! We made it. We survived three feckin' years of trainin', so we did.'

My shoulders began to shake until I too was crying with laughter. Strange glances were coming our way from all corners of the pub. My sides ached with the release of all the tension, my forehead resting on the table.

The landlord had come over from behind his bar. 'Oh, yes girls, final exams over, are they? I heard it on the grapevine – if you'll pardon me pinching the copyright.'

We nodded in unison.

'In that case,' he said, placing a half-empty bottle of gin in the middle of the table, 'you both might as well drink the rest of it. And if Matron should come in for a tipple, I'll tell her you're both off to a fancy-dress party. Enjoy it, girls, it's on the house.'

'Hello, Paola.'

Even, softly spoken tones were an intrusion into my hangover headache haze. 'So, how did it go – the final exam?' James pulled up a chair and sat, placing his cup of coffee on the table in front of him. Even that action vibrated like a thunderclap inside my head. He'd joined me in the corner of the staff dining room where I sat nursing the effects of the previous evening's gin-fest. I looked up and put on a sympathy-eliciting expression.

'Oh, I see...not so much the exam as the party afterwards. Stay right there while I fetch the cure.' He scraped his chair backwards and stood. I wanted to die. He returned a few minutes later with a mug of black coffee in one hand and a tall glass of creamy liquid in the other, then set both down in front of me and indicated the glass. 'That one first. Come on, down the hatch.'

I must have been either very trusting or extremely foolish, as after one sip, I downed the lot without a thought. It was sweet but not sickly. 'What was in that?' I asked, considering it might have been sensible to ask *before* I drank it. But then again, Shelagh and I *had* polished off a whole bottle of gin, so sense didn't really come into it.

I'd hardly seen James since the party in the social hut; the young anaesthetist I'd shamelessly snatched from Shelagh's grasp for the last dance that night. Since then it had only been during the odd cardiac arrest, when the full emergency team attended, that our paths crossed. I liked him, and it was nice to see him now – *even* through a post-binge haze. His tight, fair curly hair had been close-cropped leaving small twirls at the base of his neck. He had the softest blue eyes. Any possible relationship had faded when I went to Ireland and met Liam during my Sligo adventure, though it *was* good to see him now.

'So, what was in it?' I asked again, trying not to move my head too much, but feeling the potion working already.

'Milk, honey, vitamin C, and something to make you feel less sick. Then there's Aspirin – and a large dose of amphetamine.'

'What?' I shrieked too loudly then lowered my voice, 'I do hope you're joking.'

He grinned, amused at my consternation. 'Yes, Paola, I'm joking. No amphetamine or anything else illegal for that matter.'

'Thank God!' I began to breathe easily again.

He pointed to the mug. 'Now the coffee.'

I peered into it suspiciously. 'No cannabis?'

'None. Caffeine only. When you get pissed as often as we did as medical students, you learn a few tips along the way, especially how to recover quickly.'

I drained the coffee mug with a grimace.

'So, what did you get in the anatomy and physiology section of the paper?' asked James, his elbows resting on the table.

'Liver enzymes and the conversion of carbohydrates to glycogen, then cirrhosis and the effects of drugs and alcohol,' I said, smiling at the irony.

'Hmmm,' he raised his eyebrows, 'very apt. A lesson for us all there then.'

'In fact,' I went on, 'alcohol seemed to figure quite prominently because then I got neonates and foetal alcohol syndrome.'

'The effects on the foetus of boozing mothers-to-be.'

'Yeah, that was no problem. I'm really into neonates. It was the adult levels of trypsin and amylase I hope I got right.'

'It sounds as though you did okay.'

I sighed. 'James, I wish I had your confidence.'

'I expect you'll be all right.' He paused for a moment, thoughtfully. 'What will you do if you fail?'

That stopped me in my tracks. With a sudden horrible feeling of foreboding, I realised I hadn't given that possibility a thought.

179

I confessed there *was* no plan B. 'Does that sound totally conceited?' I asked.

'Not at all. You have to follow your dreams wherever they may take you.' He paused again. 'Can you *do* anything else?'

'Bugger off, you cheeky sod!' I retorted.

He persisted. 'But *can* you, Pao?'

I gave a huff. 'Of course I can.'

'What else *can* you do?' he asked seriously. 'Because you should *always* have a contingency plan or two.'

'I can dance a bit, sing a bit and...' I was miffed, as he was laughing now teasing me. 'I can do lots of things.' *Professional medium if all else fails*, I thought.

James put down his cup. 'Don't worry, Pao. It won't happen.' He looked at his watch. 'I must go. I'm in Theatre 2 for Millington's orthopaedic list and he's a stickler for starting promptly so...' He stood. 'Good luck. When do the results come out?'

'A month on Friday.'

'I'll look for your smiling face then.'

'Bye James.'

James' magic medicine did the trick, but now I was able to reason again and began to think. What if I *did* flunk my finals? I'd never considered the possibility – until now. Joking apart, what *would* I do? These questions kept me awake long into the night as I lay there thinking of Ireland – and Liam.

I'd written to him almost as soon as we'd returned and had grown more disappointed each day as the postman hadn't delivered an expected reply. Was I being silly? Probably. It was a holiday romance, nothing more I told myself. Maybe this genuinely nice man had felt sorry for me? That was all...wasn't it? We'd had fun and it hadn't been one-sided. I wasn't some shrinking violet who'd been taken advantage of. I'd loved every minute. *I love you, Paola.* Oh, Liam, *why* did you have to say that if you didn't mean it? Those three words slip out of mouths so easily.

I looked at the bedside clock lamenting how little time there was before the dawn broke over the far hills and I had to get up for work. I'd make myself a cup of cocoa and then a concentrated effort to clear the junk from my mind and get some sleep.

The kitchen was quiet, apart from the occasional crack of the central heating and the gentle purring of the cat in her usual spot on top of the boiler. I poured hot milk into a mug and sat at the table. Cocoa – 'chocolate' as Robbie called it in that distinctive Texan drawl of his. I smiled at memories no longer painful and sat for a short while sipping my drink and remembering things he'd said.

The way he'd called me 'Ma'am' when he was being formal or angry; 'Pao' when he wasn't being either. He'd told me about America and that I'd go there one day. I doubted it. He'd told me of his hopes and dreams and I'd told him mine.

Don't let anyone spoil your dreams, Pao. Dreams are what keep us sane in this crazy world.

It was while we'd been relaxing together, honing my so-called gift that I'd seen his death, though I didn't know it at the time.

Promise me you'll work on that remarkable ability of yours, for gifts come in so many different wrappings. Don't waste them. Tell the story. Tell it all, baby.

Suddenly I was wide awake. What had he said next? He'd looked at me steadily. Oh, and by the way, look out for the next one who calls you 'baby'. Then you can be sure that love is for real. That's how you'll know.

I dropped my mug but hardly noticed at the sudden realisation that someone else had called me that recently. Liam – it was Liam – after the attack when he'd carried me home; my tearful, bruised face resting against his soft shirt. I'd sobbed, and he'd whispered, 'Hush, you're safe now, baby.' No one had called me that since Robbie and my distress was such, I'd barely noticed at the time.

'Oh, Robbie,' I said aloud. 'If only you could have been right. But you were wrong.' It had been a while now and there'd been no word.

Hush…you're safe now, baby…baby…baby.

I went back to my room and lay awake until dawn broke.

Chapter 23

In the cold light of the new day, any further soul-searching and gnashing of teeth had to be firmly put aside.

Casualty loomed large again. The third-year student nurse on night duty had gone down with chicken pox. The irony of having to go back there was not lost on me, though I expected things would be very different. The consultant's office had a new occupant during the day: a painfully thin, sallow man called Mr Mc Allister who'd been transferred from Dundee to fill the considerable gap left by Sir Ivor. The door was now firmly closed for the night. There would be no further bellowing of 'Nurse' heard. It was not the new man's style. I expect he even put on his *own* white coat every morning, not needing the prestige of that sort of power trip. But no big personality either. No ego or established style yet.

One night, whilst passing the closed door, I paused and stood still for some moments to consider how quickly a gap is filled. It's the only way normal life can go on. Put your hand in a bucket of water then take it out and look where it had been a second ago. Nothing – that's the impression we make, and no one is expendable or irreplaceable. The space closed around Ivor's existence as sure as the water in the bucket. Tears sprang to my eyes and I swallowed the lump in my throat before hurrying back to the nightly hustle and bustle of minor injuries; the usual drunks looking for a warm place to sleep, and the fish in the tank going about their usual monotonous business.

'Friday the 13th,' I said. 'Oh, give over, Shelagh. Surely you're not *that* superstitious.'

'Yes, I am, Pao. Why do the results have to come out on *that* day, for goodness sake? Why not the day before or the day after?'

We were walking to our respective places of work the next evening – me to Casualty, and she to the male medical block. 'I know,' I teased, 'let's confound the lot of them. We'll buy a bunch of white heather from a gipsy, whilst carrying a black cat under a ladder, and not turning around three times and saying 'white rabbits' whether there's an R in the month or not.'

'Now *you're* being silly, Pao.'

I ignored her and carried on. 'Then we could accept the third light from a match – *if* we smoked and stuff our bras with four-leaf clovers. Will that satisfy you?'

She wheeled on me. 'Yer feckin' mockin' me again, Paola Green, so yer are! Two more days. I'll never survive for two more days. I can't even sleep to pass the time. I should have stayed an auxiliary nurse.'

'No, Shelagh,' I said firmly, 'you're *far* too good for that and you know it.'

'Then I wouldn't have had to suffer for these last three years. I could have gone home and spent me money every month with a lot less responsibility *and* without me head stuck in a book every night.'

I was losing patience. 'Oh, come on, Shelagh,' I chivvied, 'you don't *really* regret doing your training properly...surely?'

'Not really,' she sighed. 'I suppose if we pass, we get more money *and* they can't take your SRN away from you, can they?'

'Not unless you do something really bad. Now, come on, we'll be late.'

'Well, I still don't know how I'm goin' to get through the next two days, Pao.'

'We've no choice, Shelagh, 'it'll soon pass.' But I too was hardly sleeping. For some reason the nurses' home was unusually noisy during the day, probably high spirits in anticipation of the results. I usually gave in and got up in the early afternoons when I should have been getting much-needed restorative sleep for the night shift.

My last night on Casualty was to be a memorable one. There had been a mid-week football match at the local stadium and the 'Blues' were playing Millwall. Trouble had been expected, as fans from that club were notorious for fighting before, during and after matches. There had been a huge underestimation of just how many away-supporters would turn up – *or* the depth of feeling when they lost two-one. Fights on a grand scale had broken out.

I spent the first half of the night stitching up foreheads and knuckles, the result of thumps and 'Glasgow kisses', but by 3am we'd miraculously managed to clear the place.

Sister Beth Granger made coffee. 'Come on, Nurse, we're having a break. I'm that far from…' she made a measuring gesture with her thumb and forefinger, 'from locking the damn doors and pretending we're closed. If I have to stitch up one more foul-mouthed, cussing yobbo, I'll scream and hit him myself.' We drank in silence, our feet up on the desk.

'I'm just going for a bit of a walk in the entrance hall,' I said.

In the deserted waiting room with its white, tiled walls, it was stark, yet cosy. A few more hours and no one would be able to move in here. They'd be almost fighting for seats on the wooden benches. As well as Casualty, there would be hordes of people waiting to see the various specialists. But for now, the doors to their rooms remained closed.

My sojourn came to a halt in front of the fish tank by the blue doors of Casualty. I sprinkled in a few flakes of feed causing a short burst of excited activity before all was peaceful again.

'All things will pass.' I heard a voice from behind me and turned sharply. There was no one there and all was otherwise quiet save for the gentle hum from the tank.

All things will pass and move on, as will we, I thought. *Robbie had. Whatever fate holds in store for me – for Liam – for us, I have no control over it. Will there be any us?*

Whatever the future might bring, tomorrow was results day and so, with a gentle push they were quite unaccustomed to, I went through the blue swing doors and walked slowly towards the consultant's office at the end of the corridor. I'd stood quaking here not so very long ago, wondering whether to knock, fearing the reputation of the person on the other side.

There was no such fear now, just sadness at the passing of a brilliant mind, a soft, gentle man, whatever face he chose to present to the rest of the world. I'd come to know, if for a short time, a man who'd lived among the Inuit, who'd shared their ways, their lives, and their secrets. Since then he'd lived a solitary life – and died a solitary death. That was his wish and he was returning to a place few of us would ever know or understand. He had never told me why, and I had not asked.

Standing there quietly, I became aware of a noise – a tap-tapping from inside the room. I pressed the handle and allowed the door to swing open slowly. A cold blast of air came from the room and settled around me. I shivered, goose bumps rising on my arms. A small swishing noise came from behind the door as I stepped over the threshold.

I turned and, hanging on the back of the door by a hook, was a very large, white coat that couldn't have belonged to the new incumbent. I stood on tiptoe and reached for it. Taking it down, I held it out with its back to me like an offering: 'Your coat, Sir Ivor, but you'll have to bend down,' I said aloud. I turned towards the desk in the corner and what I saw made me drop the white coat. There on the desk was a small pool of water and in the middle of it sat a tiny, sealskin canoe, as if floating noiselessly on the ocean.

I picked it up. 'Thank you, Sir Ivor,' I said, and accepted his gift.

Chapter 24

'Get up Pao. Quickly!' Shelagh was banging on my door rousing me from much-needed sleep. 'Get up. They've been posted early – the results. It wasn't supposed to be until later this afternoon.'

Without bothering with my dressing gown, I let her in. She was hopping from one foot to the other with ill-disguised nervousness and apprehension.

'Oh God, Shelagh,' I moaned, realising it was only three hours since I'd got into bed at the end of the night shift, but my tiredness wasn't about to stop her. The momentous event that was about to unfold overtook me as I pulled on jeans and a jumper over my pyjamas.

'Oh God,' I repeated as we ran from the nurses' home to the school of nursing where a couple of dozen other young women were crowding around the notice board.

Tissie was trying her best to keep order – with limited success. In desperation, she tore down the notice. 'I will read the results for each of you *when* you all settle down and *when* I am ready,' she hollered forcefully above the chaos and clamouring. 'You will each wait your turn! Now form an orderly queue and come into my office in twos – or not at all.' The sea of bodies receded somewhat, but not before her linen cap had been knocked sideways.

Everyone queued impatiently and eventually Shelagh and I reached the front. I grabbed her hand. 'All for one?' I asked. 'Are we in this together?'

'Oh, yes, my friend. Together we stand. All girls together.'

From behind us, Jenny Parsons gave a loud shriek. 'For fuck's sake you two, shut your faces and get in there.'

Dawn is a magical time and it has never lost its wonder,

though I'd seen it far too many times on night duty, and when I'd been unable to sleep these last three years. It's as though a renewal is taking place each day. From the darkness, with its night creatures, come the first hesitant rays of light over the far horizon as a new day dawns, fresh, hopeful and filled with possibilities. From out of the gloom, the light slowly spreads across the sky. This morning, a watery sun fought for supremacy with the early autumnal, dewy chill.

I'd watched this miracle unfold many times – but not like today. Standing there in my pyjamas by the window, I looked across the manicured lawns of the nurses' home, over the dour hospital buildings to the mist-topped hills beyond. It was like the first time I'd seen it. Today, I was seeing it as a fully qualified nurse. I had passed my final exams – we all had.

Paola Green, State Registered Nurse. It felt good but weird. I didn't know any more than I did yesterday. I was no more experienced or self-assured. What *had* changed was that I was now responsible for my own actions. It was both terrifying and exciting in equal measure – a new beginning; another step on the journey, wherever that might lead. Even the new uniforms we were now entitled to wear were designed to make us feel good – dark mauve with pretty, white lace collars and a matching linen cap. My parents had bought me an antique silver buckle to adorn my new belt. I glanced at the freshly-pressed dresses waiting to go to the linen room to be shortened. We could wear them as soon as we were awarded our unique registration numbers, but they would take a few days to come through.

Both Shelagh and I had been offered jobs: me on Princess Margaret Children's Ward and she, on the new Intensive Care Unit. 'Oh, typical,' she'd said, 'all flippin' unconscious – no need for me to talk to anyone. I'd have preferred somewhere with a bit more life, so I would.'

I quickly reminded her how lucky we were. Not all of us had been offered jobs.

'And it's only for three months provisionally,' I said. 'Then, if we want, we can move on to other things.' We looked at each other and paused, realising simultaneously that we were on the verge of going our separate ways.

'Oh, Pao,' said Shelagh.

We'd been through so much together. We'd laughed, cried, got drunk and shared each other's secrets. That would remain sacrosanct forever. I think, at that moment, we both knew that. An enduring friendship had been forged, as strong as steel and one that neither of us was destined to let go in case we lost something too precious for words. An unwillingness to allow the bond to break for fear any memory should fade, hope be lost, or dream downgraded by separation.

'It's just another chapter, Pao,' Shelagh said, as if reading my thoughts. 'You have to read the end line of one story before starting another or none of it would make sense.'

I smiled sadly. 'You're right and we've finished and started quite a few, haven't we?'

She nodded and reached for my hand. 'Pao…I'm scared.'

'So am I, honey.'

She took a deep breath. 'Oh, what the hell is wrong with the two of us? We're *real* nurses now – qualified feckin' staff nurses you and me, and all the others as well. And, we are invincible…right? Say it, Pao. Say it together.'

'We are invincible,' we chorused.

'Louder!'

'We are invincible. Yeah!' we shouted, hands in the air, faces upturned to the sky, but whether either of us believed it was a different matter.

Our registration numbers allowing us to practise as trained nurses came in the post the following Friday morning, and after the weekend we were to start work as staff nurses.

Shelagh popped her head round my door after lunch. 'Pao, great news. A surprise for you – and me for that matter. A phone call came from home.'

Hope suddenly soared inside me. Could it be…?

'Mammy and Da are coming over for a few days.

'Oh, that's…wonderful,' I said, trying to hide my disappointment, though her excitement was infectious.

'They kept it a secret until now in case I failed, I suppose. Well now, there's confidence for yer.' She laughed. 'Pao, you *will* come to the station with me tonight to meet them, won't yer?'

I shook my head. 'No, Shelagh. I think they'll want their girl all to themselves at a time like this.' I didn't want to be reminded of Liam – as if I *needed* reminding. It was time to let go again, not rub salt in another open wound.

'Don't you dare stay away, Paola Green. I can go home anytime I like now *and* they asked especially that you come too. My parents fell in love with you, big style when you came to stay.'

'I brought them a load of trouble.'

'They didn't see it like that.'

'And I had a great time at their place, apart from–'

'Well, we need *not* go there,' said Shelagh firmly cutting me off. There was a pause. 'Da said Liam was asking after you.'

'Really?' I felt a sudden inner warmth at the mention of his name and the all-too-brief love affair we'd shared. Memories of the beach surged through my body like a fire. 'I don't suppose I'll ever see him again.'

Shelagh shook her head. 'You don't know that.'

I clasped fingertips to my brow. 'Oh, Shelagh, I'm here and he's in Sligo – and I'm a realist. Holiday romances *never* come to anything – you must realise that. He's never written or phoned. Love doesn't travel well when you're separated. I really would have liked to have heard from him, but he hasn't contacted me since we left.'

Shelagh shook her head. 'I suppose you're right. Oh, Pao, I'm so looking forward to seein' me folks, I am. Say you'll come.'

I sighed. 'All right then. It'll be lovely to see them again.'

'Good grief!' She consulted her watch. 'We only have three hours to get ready.'

'What?' I said. 'I've known you get ready in five minutes flat if the prospect of a night out suddenly presented itself – *and* you managed to look fabulous.'

She laughed again. 'Well, I don't want to meet me mammy lookin like a feckin' trash can, do I? She always looks immaculate, so you'd better make the effort too.'

I recalled how Astrid always managed to look as though she'd just stepped off the catwalk no matter what she was doing. 'We're going to need every minute of those three hours,' I said. 'Come on, Shelagh. Stop talking and let's get going.'

Dusk was falling as we reached the Midland Station and, after a few minutes, the usual garbled announcement heralded the train's arrival. On the platform, people grabbed their luggage and surged forward in preparation to board. We craned our necks as the train pulled in and the doors began to open, scanning each carriage for a glimpse.

'Can you see them?' I shouted above the noise of the guard's whistle.

'Not yet, but Da likes to be towards the back of the train. He says it's like aeroplanes. They don't often back into things.'

The crush of bodies began to disperse and there, right at the end of the platform were Astrid and Eoghan standing close together and waving furiously. We waved back just as frantically. The train pulled away on its journey and the platform cleared. In the stillness that followed, Shelagh suddenly began to sing. 'Will you dance if I asked you, in the fast-fading light...?'

I gave her a sharp look of disbelief. It was cruel and insensitive, and I couldn't believe what she was doing. She looked at me and raising her eyebrows, carried on – and then I heard another voice join hers. 'Would you dance in my arms, love? Will you stay with me tonight?'

Astrid and Eoghan parted, and there, standing behind them, was Liam singing at the top of his voice. I turned to Shelagh with a gasp, my eyes wide.

'Go on,' she said, giving me a prod with her finger. 'Run.'

'Yes...but which way?' I whispered somehow rooted to the spot, suddenly fearful and uncertain.

'You know very well which way, Pao.' she said. 'Now run.'

Liam held out his arms, and turning towards him, I ran.

THE END

If you have enjoyed this book, we recommend these books, also by the same author:

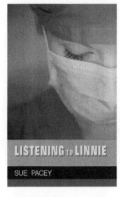

Listening to Linnie, the first of the 'Linnie' trilogy (the third book is currently in preparation).

ISBN 978-1-909813-04-5
£7.99

A Silent Cradle, a story based on real lives in the Second World War.

ISBN 978-1-909813-29-8
£9.49

All books available from Bannister Publications Ltd
118 Saltergate, CHESTERFIELD, S40 1NG

www.bannisterpublications.com

01246 440558